BAVARIAN SUNSET

BAVARIAN SUNSET

James Pattinson

ROBERT HALE · LONDON

ISBN 978-0-7090-8407-5

Robert Hale Limited
Clerkenwell House
Clerkenwell Green
London EC1R 0HT

www.halebooks.com

2 4 6 8 10 9 7 5 3 1

Printed and bound in Great Britain by
Biddles Limited, King's Lynn

Contents

ONE

Fortune of War

The boy first saw the vehicle when it was some two or three hundred yards away. It was not very clearly defined, for there was a curtain of mist hanging around where the roadway emerged from the trees, making visibility poor. Though in theory winter should have been past, spring was proving slow to establish itself and there was still snow on the ground. Winters could be long and bitter in this part of Germany, and this one had been particularly so in more senses than one, for the Third Reich was collapsing in chaos; Hitler's boasted Thousand Year Reich was tumbling into ruin about the ears of its Nazi architect and the invaders were storming in from the east and the west.

The boy was scarcely old enough to appreciate what was happening to his country. But if he did not understand the causes, he knew what the consequences of war could be. He had witnessed some of its effects when they had been living in the house in Berlin; but as the bombing became worse his mother had left the capital, taking him with her to the family estate in Lower Saxony.

His father, an officer in a crack panzer regiment, was

already dead; killed in action somewhere in the bleak wastes of the Russian front. This fact had been revealed to him in an oblique way to spare him as much as possible of the pain, but he had gradually come to accept this bereavement and the knowledge that he would never see his father again. He was affected less than might have been expected by the loss of a parent; his mother was still with him and that was enough; she was the central figure in his life.

At first life in the big house on the estate had been pleasant enough. It had been peaceful and there had been servants to ensure that things ran smoothly. But the numbers of these employees steadily decreased as the men were pressed into service in the armed forces and the women departed to work in factories or on the land. Soon only a few old retainers were left.

And now even they were gone. The war was coming ever closer, advancing like an irresistible tide from the west, and people were fleeing from it as the contagion of fear took hold upon their minds. The boy's mother could have left also, taking him with her; she had been urged to do so, but had refused. Where would they have gone? There was no refuge left. Better to stay here and wait for the Americans or the British than to flee to the east and be caught by the Russian barbarians. One could at least feel sure of civilised treatment from the Allies.

So they had been alone now for two weeks in this chilly echoing mansion with its deserted rooms, waiting for whatever might come. All around the land showed white under its thin covering of snow, and the clumps of pine trees stood as if huddling together for warmth.

The boy, watching from a window in the house, saw the vehicle approaching and becoming clearer in outline. It was quite small; drab in colour and not armoured: just a light truck with canvas-covered back. Halfway to the house it stopped and a man got out. He appeared to be using a pair of binoculars to study the building and its surroundings. After a while he lowered the glasses and got back into the truck, which moved forward again at a steady pace.

The boy kept his eyes on it as it came up to the house and stopped again. He had a feeling of uneasiness; it might have been a presentiment, of evil perhaps; he could not explain it. Somehow this small brown-painted vehicle with its spattering of mud and its dented wings held more menace than an entire column of armoured cars and troop-carriers would have done. He had an impulse to run and hide, but he remained where he was.

Two men got out of the truck. They were in khaki battledress, one a burly thickset man, the other slimmer and taller. They seemed to confer for a moment or so, looking towards the porticoed front of the house; then they began to walk towards it and the boy lost sight of them.

He left his place by the window and went to the door of the room, which opened on to the spacious entrance hall. He opened the door slightly so that he could peer through the gap, and he saw the two men walk into the hall. They had not bothered to ring the bell or knock, but the front door had not been locked and there had been nothing to check them. They entered warily; the thickset man was carrying a submachine-gun and the other man, who was younger and appeared almost boyish in comparison, had an automatic pistol in his hand. The older man had three stripes on his sleeves and the younger had two cloth stars on each shoulder-strap. If the boy had been better acquainted with military uniforms he would have realised that he was seeing for the first time in his life a lieutenant and a sergeant of the British Army. He heard the sergeant make some remark to the lieutenant and heard the officer reply, but he could not understand the words that were spoken.

The two men advanced further into the hall, and at that moment the boy's mother appeared at the head of the broad stairway which led to the upper floors. The two men saw her and came to a halt, watching her as she made the descent. She reached the foot of the stairs and stood there with one hand resting lightly on the newel. She addressed the intruders in German.

'Who are you? What do you want?'

Neither man appeared to understand the language.

'Do you speak English?' the lieutenant asked.

She nodded. 'Yes.'

'Good. It will make things simpler. Are you the lady of the house?'

'Yes. I am Frau Neuberg.'

The lieutenant gazed at her with interest. She was an attractive woman, blonde and slender, not yet thirty years old. Any man would have given her more than a second glance. The sergeant's gaze was fixed on her too, and the expression on his rugged face was unmistakably lecherous.

'Who else is there in the house?' the lieutenant asked.

'Only my son.'

'Your son?'

'A small boy.'

'Ah! And your husband?'

'Captain Neuberg is dead. He was killed in action in Russia some time ago.'

The lieutenant gave a shrug. 'The fortune of war.'

'As you say, the fortune of war. Or perhaps the misfortune.'

'There are servants, possibly?'

'There were, but they have gone.' Frau Neuberg repeated her original question in English: 'Who are you?'

The lieutenant stowed his pistol in the webbing holster attached to his belt. 'Oh,' he said, 'I fancy you already know that well enough. You must have been expecting us to come to you eventually even in this backwater. We are the British Army.'

'Just the two of you?'

'At the moment. A small detachment, you might say. Scouting. Later no doubt there will be others.'

'And your names?'

'There is no need for you to know them. Let us for the present remain anonymous.'

The sergeant gave a smirk and said: 'No names, no pack-drill. Right?'

The boy, unable to understand what was being said, had edged into the hall, encouraged by the presence of his mother. The sergeant spotted him.

'Well, look who's here! The man of the house. Come right in, kid. Join the party.'

He made a beckoning gesture and the boy advanced a few steps, then stopped, glancing at his mother for guidance. She spoke to him, and he ran to her and took her hand.

'So this is your son?' the lieutenant said.

'Yes.'

'Fine boy. Your only child?'

'Yes.'

'You must be very fond of him. Wouldn't want anything bad to happen to him, I imagine?'

She looked puzzled, sensing some hidden meaning in the words, and uneasy.

'Why should anything bad happen to him?'

'No reason at all. If you're sensible. As I am sure you are.'

'What do you mean by sensible?'

'Co-operative, shall we say?'

She looked hard at him. 'What do you want of me?'

The sergeant laughed. 'What does any man want of a woman? Specially a woman as tasty as you, lady.'

'No,' she said; still looking at the lieutenant and not the sergeant. 'You wouldn't.'

'Oh, wouldn't he?' the sergeant said. 'Just because he's an officer and a gentleman, as the saying is, don't go kidding yourself. Officers and gentlemen are just like the rest of us when you get down to the basics. They want their oats, and when the chance comes they take it pronto.'

The lieutenant said, addressing the woman: 'Suppose you and I were to have a little talk, tête-à-tête. Suppose we go upstairs and leave the boy with the sergeant. What do you say?'

The woman shook her head. 'No.'

The lieutenant touched the butt of the holstered pistol with his fingers. 'We have the means to enforce our will. For your son's sake if not for your own, don't make things difficult. Surely you can see it would be pointless.'

Still she hesitated. She might have been reflecting how young the lieutenant seemed. There was a cherubic look about him which was belied by his words and his manner. He was like a mischievous schoolboy who had been given a little brief authority and was taking a malicious pleasure in exercising it. In this situation he was all-powerful; a god; or a devil.

'Do you wish for a demonstration?' He glanced at the sergeant. 'Show her what the gun can do.'

It was ten minutes later when the lieutenant appeared at the head of the stairs. The woman was not with him. He came down slowly, dabbing at his left cheek with a handkerchief. It could be seen when he came nearer that there was blood on the cheek.

'So,' the sergeant remarked, 'she used her claws?'

'Never mind what she used.' The lieutenant spoke testily, and it was evident that he was not in the best of tempers. The knuckles of his right hand were also bleeding from abrasions on the skin. 'Damned bitch!'

The sergeant grinned sardonically. 'What'd you do to get her dander up?'

'It's none of your damned business.'

'If you say so. Do we go now, sir?'

'Not yet. I mean to have compensation for this.' The lieutenant indicated his scratched cheek and glanced at the sergeant's haversack. 'I don't imagine you've been idle in that line.'

The sergeant shrugged. 'I've picked up a few souvenirs. Spoils of war, as the saying is.'

'I'll bet you have. Well, stay here. I'm going to take a look around.'

'What about the kid? Do I let him go?'

'Him? Oh, I suppose so. What harm can he do?'

The sergeant had already relinquished his grip on the boy, but he was standing between him and the stairway, making it impossible for him to pass. The boy had not made any attempt to do so; he was too much in fear of this hard-faced man who could have crushed him with a blow of the fist. After the one scream there had been no more sound audible from the upper floor, and then the officer had appeared with blood on his cheek and knuckles. The boy wanted to run to his mother but was held by his fear of the men, especially the older one.

But now the sergeant stepped aside and made a gesture with his hand. 'You're free, kid. Beat it.'

He understood the gesture if not the words; he was being told that he could go. Without a word on his own part he took the hint and darted up the stairs. He knew which room to go to, and the door had been left slightly ajar, the lieutenant not having bothered to close it completely on leaving.

The boy halted at the door. He had been prepared to rush into the room, but now he hesitated, checked by some premonition of what he might find inside. There was no sound coming from within; he listened intently but could detect nothing, not even the hint of any movement. It frightened him, this utter silence.

But he plucked up his courage and pushed the door a little wider open and went inside. The sight that met his eyes shocked him as never before. It was a shock that was to remain with him throughout his life; a picture painted so vividly on his mind that it could never be erased, however much time might elapse. It was there for ever, a nightmare vision so horrifying to a boy of his tender age that it was as if it were burned into his consciousness with a white-hot iron.

She was lying on the bed, on her back, her eyes closed, her face bruised and bloody, her lips cut, pulpy and swollen. She was wearing nothing but a torn slip, and this was rucked up to her waist. Her legs were spreadeagled, and in the angle between them was a little mat of hair which the boy had never seen before, had never dreamed existed.

He shivered, but not with the cold, though the bedroom was frigid. He felt as if he were trespassing on forbidden territory, seeing what he ought never to have been allowed to see. It was as though he were committing some unspeakable crime in looking at his mother as she was at this moment.

But then, overwhelming all other feeling, came the thought that she was dead. He gave a wail of anguish and ran to the bed and threw himself on the body, his eyes blinded with tears; crying out to her, imploring her to come back to him, not to leave him; praying for a miracle to happen that would restore her to life.

And after a minute or two it seemed that his prayers were answered. She gave a sigh and her eyes opened. She appeared confused at first, unable for a few moments to appreciate what had happened. But the moments quickly passed and memory came flooding back. She became aware of the condition she was in and made a movement to pull the slip down over the nakedness of the lower half of her body.

'Oh, mama!' the boy cried, with a sob in his voice. 'I thought you were dead.'

She managed a wan smile and spoke reassuringly through the cut and swollen lips. 'No, not dead. Don't cry, my darling. It is nothing. Nothing for you to cry about.'

He had drawn back from her, sensing again that feeling of shame at seeing her like this. She seemed to be aware of his embarrassment and was herself embarrassed. She managed to draw a quilt over her body.

'Those men,' she said. 'Have they gone?'

'I don't know.' He stared at her, at her bruised and blood-smeared face, eyes wide and questioning. 'Why?'

She guessed his meaning. Why had the man attacked her like this? She was not sure she knew the answer herself. It was as if a sudden madness had taken possession of him, a kind of bestiality. She had not resisted him at first; it would have been senseless. But then … Had he meant to kill her? Had he believed her dead before he left her? Or had he stopped on the brink, drawn back from that ultimate crime? Who could tell?

'I will kill him,' the boy said. He knew it was the lieutenant who had done this to his mother, though he did not understand why. He felt a burning hatred of the man; it possessed him completely. He clenched his fists. 'I will kill him. I will, I will.'

'No,' the woman said. 'You are too young. Too small. You must forget what happened. Put it out of your mind.'

Forget! How could he forget the unforgettable? The memory would remain with him always. He felt the frustration of the child, lacking the strength to do what he would have done had he been older. He had a desire to do the deed now, but he knew that he could not, that he would have to wait until the years gave him the power. Well, he would wait; but some day, some day he would take revenge.

He heard the sound of a motor starting up, and he ran to the window and looked out. Below him the small brown truck was turning in a half-circle. Then it began to move away down the approach road, making new tracks on the thin layer of snow. He watched it go, carrying away the two men who had come out of nowhere to break so brutally into his young life and now were going away he knew not where. He did not even know their names. How then could he ever hope to find them again? How could it possibly be done? And yet he must do it, sometime, somehow, come what might.

'I will kill him,' he said.

It was a vow.

*   *   *

'You will say nothing to anyone,' the lieutenant said. 'Not a word. You understand?'

The sergeant gave a laugh. 'You reckon I would? I'm not that stupid. I got myself to think about too.'

The two men were in the truck, driving away from the big house. Soon it would be lost to sight behind them. They might never see it again, but the memory of it would go with them. The blood had dried on the lieutenant's cheek, but he looked morose and unhappy; possibly ashamed. The sergeant's words had emphasised the link between them; the criminal link which made each of them dependent on the other's discretion. They were both looters, and he was something else besides, something far worse. And the sergeant knew. Which put him in the man's power. He did not like the thought of that. What had possessed him to do what he had done? A devil inside him? Maybe so. He regretted it now; not from remorse; he felt nothing of that kind; but because it had given the sergeant this hold upon him.

'I suppose you got what you wanted?' the sergeant said.

The lieutenant glanced at him sharply. 'What do you mean?'

'Why that what you pinched. What else would I mean?' The man was grinning; it was obvious that he was well aware of the thought that had immediately flashed into his companion's mind. But he had been talking about something else. 'Me, I wouldn't go for nothing like that. Meanter say, what's it worth?'

'Never mind what it's worth.' The lieutenant was not at all sure himself. It had been a spur of the moment decision, hastily taken because he was eager to get away from the house without further delay. Perhaps it would have been wiser to have left empty-handed; but even if he had there would still have been that other thing to put him in the sergeant's hands. There would have been no way of wiping that out, even though the man did not know the whole of it and could only guess.

'Well,' the sergeant said, 'this bloody war will be over before long now. Jerry's on the run good and proper. Soon we'll be back in civvy street and it'll be goodbye to all this.' He gave the lieutenant a sly look. 'You and me, I reckon we oughter keep in touch. We're two of a kind. There'll be openings for a pair like us. Wotcher say?'

The lieutenant said nothing.

'Think about it.'

The lieutenant was thinking about it, and his thoughts were gloomy.

TWO

Miss Hoffman

'What do you think of it?' the girl asked. 'Honestly.'

She was blonde and she spoke with something of a foreign accent. Sam Grant looked carefully at the picture and carefully at the girl standing beside him. It was advisable to be careful in situations such as this, because there was no telling whether or not you were speaking to the originator of the painting. In a gallery of this kind artists tended to hover near their own productions in the hope of picking up a few compliments – or maybe even a sale.

So he answered a trifle warily: 'Did you paint it?'

She could have, he thought; she looked the artistic type: rather casually dressed, as though she had picked up just what came to hand and thrown it on without a second thought. But of course this might have been misleading; the whole operation might have been very carefully planned with an eye to its overall effect. Planned or not, the result was stunning. And she was pretty stunning herself, no doubt about it: possibly twenty-eight years old or so, tallish and well con-structed, with classic features. Altogether worth a second glance and maybe more.

She smiled, as though the suggestion amused her. 'No. You'll be perfectly safe in giving a candid opinion.'

'Candidly then, I think it's a con.'

'Con?'

'A confidence trick. It's just a piece of canvas with splodges of paint thrown at it haphazard. It's rubbish; but of course nobody dare say so for fear of being labelled an ignoramus or a philistine.'

'You aren't afraid to say so, though.'

'No. But I'm not a member of the club. It makes no difference to me what people think about my tastes in art.'

'I suppose not. Although I imagine there might be occasions when some knowledge in that line might be useful for a private investigator. Isn't that so, Mr Grant?'

Grant was startled. 'So you know who I am?'

'Oh, yes.'

'Who told you?'

'Someone. I've forgotten for the moment just who it was.'

He did not believe that. It had to be Cynara; that was why she had insisted on his accompanying her to this exhibition. It was all a put-up job to steer him in the direction of a prospective client. She was a great one for devious manoeuvres like this to whip up business for The Samuel Grant Inquiry Agency. Which was no doubt understandable, seeing that he and she were living together and without clients for the agency there would be a regrettable lack of money to keep her in the style to which she was accustomed. Not that there was anything at all grand about this style at the best of times, but at the worst of them it was apt to become a question of keeping the wolf from the door with anything that came to hand.

Like this blonde, maybe.

'Do you think,' she said, 'that we could go somewhere and have a heart-to-heart talk?'

'About what precisely?'

'Business, for example.'

'That's a good example. But there's a difficulty.'

'What kind of difficulty?'

'I'm with someone.'

'Of course you are. With Cynara. But she won't mind. It was her idea really.'

So it was as he had suspected. It had been arranged.

And at that moment Miss Jones herself joined them. 'Ah!' she said. 'I see you two have become acquainted. That's fine.'

'Well, not entirely acquainted,' Grant said. 'I don't yet know who I've been talking to.'

'Oh,' the blonde said, 'I should have told you. I am Gerda Hoffmann.'

'Well, how do you do, Miss Hoffman?'

'I'm very well, thank you.' She turned to Cynara. 'He doesn't like this picture.'

Cynara studied it for a few moments and came up with her considered opinion. 'It's got something. I can't quite put my finger on it, but it definitely has got something.'

'It's called paint,' Grant said. 'Should we go?'

* * *

They talked while drinking and eating the kind of sugary and creamy pastries that were regarded with horror by the health gang. They were guaranteed to rot the teeth and block up the arteries. But they were of course delicious.

'So how did you two come to know each other?' Grant asked.

'Oh,' Cynara said, 'we met in Austria years ago. We were both on a skiing holiday. We've kept in touch. So when Gerda happened to be in London she looked me up. She has a problem, you see. And I told her I thought you could help.'

Grant looked at Miss Hoffmann. 'A problem?'

'Yes.'

All round them people were stoking up their bodies with light refreshment and there was a continual tinkle of crockery and a hum of conversation set against a background of subdued music which seemed to emanate from nowhere in particular but was possibly oozing from the walls by a kind of tonal osmosis.

'What kind of problem?'

She hesitated a moment, as though debating in her mind the question of where to begin. Then she said: 'Two weeks ago a painting was sold at a London auction. I wish to find out who entered it in the sale.'

'Wouldn't the simplest way of doing that have been to go and ask the auctioneers?'

'I did that, but they refused to tell me.'

'Why? Did they give any reason?'

'Oh, yes. They said it was because the vendor wished to remain anonymous and they were bound to respect his wishes. According to them it was a question of professional etiquette.'

Grant thought he had heard that one before; it was a common excuse for not divulging information, much used by journalists and people in his own particular line of business. On occasion he had made use of it himself.

'Who,' he asked, 'are these auctioneers?'

'Lingarten and Son.'

'Ah!'

'You've heard of them?'

'Yes, I've heard of them.'

The fact was that Lingarten's had something of a reputation for sailing pretty close to the wind. Things came up for sale at the Beldon Lane Auction Rooms which more reputable firms might have looked at askance. The whisper was that they were not too strict in applying the normal rules of provenance regarding the items of art and antiquity which they accepted for auction.

'This painting,' he said. 'What is it? An important work?'

'Not particularly. It's called *Bavarian Sunset* and it's by a German artist named Arnold Sempler who was accused of decadence by the Nazis. He also had the misfortune to be a Jew and was sent to Belsen, where he died. Since the war there's been something of a revival in his reputation and his work has been rather sought after, particularly by American collectors. He's never got into the big league or anything like that, but his pictures have fetched useful prices. But perhaps you knew that?'

Grant shook his head. 'No. I have to admit that my knowledge of art – and especially German art – is strictly limited. The fact is I'd never heard of Sempler until this moment. But what's your interest in the picture? I mean why do you want to know who the vendor was?'

For some reason or other she seemed unwilling to enlighten him on this point. 'For the present I don't think there is any need to go into that. Later perhaps I'll tell you the whole story, but not now. The question is, do you think you can do this job for me? I'm prepared, of course, to pay whatever your fee may be.'

Grant liked the sound of that. Evidently she was not

expecting to get cut-rate terms on the strength of her friendship with Cynara.

'Well,' he said, 'it may not be easy if the auctioneers are not willing to give the information.'

At which point Cynara butted in pretty sharply. 'My God, Sam, don't be so gloomy.' She turned to Gerda. 'He's always like this; a born pessimist if ever there was one, ever ready to look on the black side of things. But he's very clever really, you know.'

'Oh, I'm sure of it.'

Grant felt slightly embarrassed by this rather over-enthusiastic piece of advocacy. But it was Miss Jones's way; she was always ready at the drop of a hat to proclaim his outstanding abilities as a private investigator. And he wished she wouldn't sometimes. He gave an apologetic smile, excusing himself.

'She's biased, of course.'

He would have made a guess that his two companions were much the same age, which was too far below his own for his peace of mind. He was prey to a constant fear that one day Cynara would tire of living with him in his dingy flat in Kilburn and take off for more salubrious quarters with a younger and maybe richer man. So far, it had to be admitted, she had shown no inclination to do so, but this was no guarantee that she never would, and the possibility that she might bothered him not a little. What, after all, did a none too successful private eye, knocking forty and not much of a contender in the male beauty stakes, have to offer a girl like her? Not a hell of a lot, if the truth were told.

Apart from the matter of age there was not much similarity between the two young women: Cynara, with her flame-red hair and light dusting of freckles, was lovely enough to attract any man, but Gerda had a different kind of beauty which might perhaps have been described as being of the Nordic type, pale golden hair and ice-blue eyes that were not perhaps without a trace of hardness in them.

'So,' she said, 'what are you telling me? That you can or cannot obtain the information I am looking for?'

'I can't guarantee anything, but if you want me to I'll do my best to find the answer.'

'And his best is the best there is,' Cynara assured her.

It was not strictly true; she was exaggerating again. But Grant let it pass.

'Then it's settled,' Gerda said. 'You will do what you can.'

'I'll do what I can.'

*   *   *

The next morning he was in Beldon Lane, which was one of those London byways that still had a Victorian flavour about them; very narrow, very dingy, and with a number of rather curious businesses occupying the ancient buildings on either side. Lingarten's was one of them. The entrance gave no evidence of a prosperous establishment within; it was as unimpressive as all the other entrances along the lane, and only a tarnished brass plate on the right bearing the name of the firm indicated to Grant that he had come to the right place.

There was an alleyway at one side which apparently gave access to a rear entrance, and as Grant came to a halt on the pavement a man in a grey dust-coat came out of the alleyway and unloaded a tea-chest from the back of a light van that was parked by the kerb. With this burden he re-entered the alleyway and Grant followed him.

A few paces took the grey-coated man to an open doorway. He went inside, and Grant, still following, found himself in a large fusty room where a number of crates and stacks of framed pictures and objects of various other kinds were stored, no doubt waiting their turn to be sold in an adjoining saleroom. The man in the dust-coat, who was middle-aged and stringy, with a receding hair line, set the tea-chest down, turned about and noticed for the first time that he was not alone.

'Here!' he said. 'Who are you? How did you get in?'

'I followed you,' Grant said.

The man looked at him suspiciously. He had a scrawny neck and a prominent Adam's-apple and not much chin to speak of. His eyes had a slight squint in them.

'Why?'

'I'd like to have a little talk with you.'

'Talk? What would you want to talk to me about?'

'A picture.'

'Aw, come off it. What would I know about pictures? I'm just a flippin' handler. I carry 'em but I don't know nothin' about 'em. I leave all that to the experts.'

'I'm sure you do. But I expect you know what comes in, don't you?'

'Well, I may do. But I still don't see –'

'There was a particular one came in recently and was sold by auction. *Bavarian Sunset*, painted by a German artist name Arnold Sempler. Do you remember handling it?'

The man in the dust-coat answered warily: 'I might. What about it?'

'I'd like to know who the vendor was. The person who entered it for sale.'

'So why come to me? Why don't you go to the office by

the front entrance and ask there?'

'Because they wouldn't tell me if I did.'

'Why not?'

'Because the vendor wishes to remain anonymous.'

'They told you that?'

'No. It was somebody else who asked, and that was the answer they gave.'

'That's it then, innit? Your bad luck, mate.'

'Perhaps. But if some other person could give me the information it might be worth his while. You get my meaning?'

It was obvious that the man did. He sucked his teeth, squinted hard at Grant and appeared to come to a decision. 'Look, mate, I got work to do right now, but I'll be knocking off for lunch at one o'clock. Meet me in the Red Lion. Know where that is? Just round the corner.'

'Yes, I know.'

'Okay then. Be seein' you.'

* * *

The Red Lion was an unassuming public-house not far from the auction rooms. Grant's companion, who had exchanged his dust-coat for a well-worn tweed jacket and whose name turned out to be Sid Biggs, lunched off sandwiches and beer, seated opposite his interrogator at a small marble-topped table. Grant paid for the beer and sandwiches, eating nothing himself but drinking beer too.

'So,' Biggs said, 'what's your interest in that there picture?'

'I am acting for a client who wishes to know just where it came from.'

'A client, you say?' The word seemed to add to Biggs's suspicion. He cast a glance round the room, which was fairly crowded at that time of day, and lowered his voice to a conspiratorial level, as if fearful of being overheard. 'So what are you? A private eye or something of that kind?'

'Something of the kind.'

'And why would this here client want to know the answer to your question?'

'I can't tell you that.'

'Can't or won't?'

'Never mind which. It's not of any interest to you.'

'I don't know so much about that.' Biggs took a mouthful of sandwich and chewed it, looking at Grant reflectively. 'And I don't know as how I oughter be talking to you really. Meanter say, I could be making trouble for meself.'

'I doubt it. Who's to know you've even had contact with me? I'm not going to broadcast the fact.'

'Well that may be so. But suppose I was to give you a bit of the info, what would there be in it for me?'

Grant took a wallet from his pocket and extracted a twenty-pound note, which he laid on the table. Biggs glanced at it and then gave a shake of the head.

'Not enough. There's the risk to take into account, see?'

Grant extracted another twenty-pound note from the wallet and laid it on top of the first, consoling himself with the thought that it would all go down on the expense account when it was presented to Miss Hoffmann. He just hoped she was as well heeled as she appeared to be. She had given him a generous retainer, so the omens were favourable.

'That's the limit,' he said. 'Now tell me.'

'Well,' Biggs said, 'it's like this here; I ain't taken into the confidence of the bosses, so I don't get to know all as goes on around here. They don't give me a list of the names and addresses of the clients and that.'

'I didn't imagine they would. But you know something, don't you? Otherwise you wouldn't be talking to me now.'

'That's true,' Biggs admitted.

'So what do you know? Out with it.'

Biggs took a pull at his mug of beer, wiped his mouth with the back of his hand, gave a cough and said: 'I know who brought that picture in, because I seen him.'

'So it was someone familiar to you?'

'Oh, yes. Quite a regular, as you might say.'

'And his name?'

'Walter Munnet.'

'The antiques dealer?'

'Yes.'

'Aha!'

'You've heard of him?'

'Oh, I've heard of him all right. You're quite sure that's who it was?'

'Sure, I'm sure. Couldn't mistake a phiz as ugly as his. Walked in with the picture under his arm. Wrapped in brown paper, it was, and tied up with string.'

'If it was wrapped up how did you know what it was?'

'Because I had to take it into the storeroom after they took the paper off, di'n't I?'

'So let's get this straight. You're absolutely certain it was Walter Munnet who brought the item in?'

'How many times do I have to tell you? Of course I'm certain. I'd take an oath on it.'

'He may have been acting for a third party.'

'Well, that's as may be. It's up to you to ask him. I've told you what I know. Now do I get the money?'

'Take it,' Grant said.

Biggs shot out a hand and took it.

THREE

A Man Named Peck

'An antiques dealer!' Gerda said. And Grant could tell that this was not quite what she had wished to hear. She sounded surprised and disappointed.

'I'm afraid so.'

They were sitting in Grant's office, which was a rather sparsely furnished room just above a fishmonger's shop in Shepherd's Bush. It was hardly the kind of place to impress prospective clients, and he could guess from the expression on Miss Hoffmann's face when she walked in that she was not impressed; not favourably anyway. But it was where he had arranged to meet her to report progress, and that was where she was, sitting on one of the hard wooden chairs and looking at him across the battered kneehole desk on which was the telephone answering machine that unfortunately attracted less custom than he might have hoped.

Cynara was there too. She acted as his part-time secretary and gave a hand with the clerical work, such as it was, besides steering any likely customers in his direction whenever the opportunity occurred.

'But surely an antiques dealer would sell direct to the buyer, wouldn't he? Not through an auction house.

Doesn't he have a shop?'

'Oh, he has one. But I imagine a man like Walter Munnet would figure that some of the things coming into his hands might fetch a better price at auction. And he could have been looking for a quick sale to get the thing off his hands.'

'I see.' Gerda Hoffmann looked thoughtful. 'This doesn't get us very far, does it?'

'You mean Munnet isn't the man you're looking for?'

'I'm quite certain he isn't. We must do some more searching. Or rather you must. We need to discover who he got the painting from. You can do that?'

'Again,' Grant said, 'I can try. But I've no doubt he'll be cagey.'

'Cagey? I don't think I know the word.'

'Secretive. Unwilling to divulge the information. I've had dealings with friend Walter and he's a dodgy customer. Plays his cards very close to his chest.'

'Then you'll just have to winkle the information out of him, won't you, Sam?' Cynara remarked. And turning to Gerda: 'He'll manage it. Look at the way he found out about this Munnet creature. Didn't take him long, did it?'

'No, it didn't.'

'So you see. He's quite a wizard really.'

'I am not a wizard,' Grant said. 'I simply ask questions and try to get the right answers.' He spoke to Gerda. 'I suppose you're still not going to tell me why you want to find this person you're looking for?'

'Not yet. For the present I think it is best if you do not know. Later perhaps –'

Grant failed to see why she should be so guarded, but if she wished it to be that way she was entitled to. She was the client; she was paying the piper and had a right

to call the tune whichever way it might please her to do
so.

*   *   *

Walter Munnet's place of business might have served as
the setting for a film of Dickens's 'The Old Curiosity
Shop'. In fact it had probably been there in Dickensian
times. There was an aged look about it, and when you
stepped inside you were met by an odour of ancient
things which seemed to emanate from the very fabric of
the objects arrayed for sale within. The light was dim,
even at midday, so you peered as if into a darkened
tunnel where hazy, ill-defined shapes resolved themselves on closer inspection into chests of drawers and
run-down grandfather clocks and brass coal-scuttles
and warming-pans and the like.

Munnet himself was almost as much a caricature of a
man as an illustration by Phiz or Cruikshank. He was
small and thin and stooping; indeed, there was so little
of him that it might have been imagined that a strong
gust of wind could have swept him away. His face was
wrinkled and the skin had a yellowish tinge, whitened
here and there by a sprouting of stubble. His head was
stone-bald and the temples appeared to have been
gouged into hollows by a sculptor's knife; but his eyes
were bright and intelligent, if a trifle shifty. He was
dressed in a rusty black suit which hung on him loosely,
as though it had retained its original size while he had
gradually shrunk inside it with the passing of the years.

He was on his guard as soon as he saw who it was who
had walked into the shop. As he had told Miss
Hoffmann, Grant had had dealings with him in the
past, but never as a customer for the goods on show. In

fact his acquaintanceship with Walter Munnet went all the way back to the days when he had been a detective constable in the Metropolitan Police; and that was longer ago than he cared to remember.

'Why, if it ain't Mr Grant!' Munnet said. 'It's a long time since I last saw you. This is an unexpected pleasure.'

Grant did not believe for a moment that his visit was giving the antiques dealer any pleasure. Munnet's display of affability was just a front.

'We all get surprises, Walter. It's what makes life so interesting.'

Munnet gave a rather twisted grin. 'Maybe so, maybe so. And to what am I indebted for this visit? Wouldn't be just a social call for old time's sake would it? You're not here simply to pass the time of day, I suppose?'

'No, Walter, I'm not. Much as I enjoy having a bit of a chinwag with you, that's not what brings me here right now.'

'Thought not. And I don't imagine you're looking for something to buy for a lady friend. You never did buy nothing off me as far as I can remember and I'm not expecting you to start now.'

'Then you won't be disappointed.'

'So it has to be other business. Well, you'd better come into the office. It'll be more private.'

As far as Grant could see there was no one else in the shop to overhear any conversation they might have; trade seemed to be very slack. But nevertheless he allowed himself to be conducted to the little room at the back which served as an office. A pimply youth was already in there pretending to be doing some work at a rickety desk, but Munnet dismissed him with orders to mind the shop, and he sidled out without uttering a word.

'Now,' Munnet said, 'what's on your mind?'

'I'm looking for information.'

Munnet seemed to become even more guarded on hearing this, as if summoning up mental rein-forcements to man the ramparts.

'Ah!'

'Regarding a certain painting.'

'Painting! What painting?'

'One called *Bavarian Sunset* by an artist named Arnold Sempler, a German Jew who died in a Nazi concentration camp.'

'Never heard of him,' Munnet said.

Grant gave an admonishing wag of the finger. 'Oh dear me! What a little fibber you are! Or have you got a very short memory? Don't you remember that quite recently you entered this picture of his for an art auction at Lingarten and Son's?'

'Who told you that?'

'Never mind who told me; let's just say I know. You're not going to deny it, are you?'

Munnet shrugged resignedly. 'Wouldn't be no point, would there? Looks like you nosied out the fact somehow; and you shouldn't have been able to. I'll be having a word or two with Lingarten's about that. They agreed to keep it confidential.'

'Why all the secrecy?'

'That's my business.'

'And my guess is it could be pretty shady business at that.'

'You can guess what you like. Makes no difference.'

'No? I think it does; I think it makes a lot of difference. So now I'm going to ask you where you got the picture.'

'That's confidential information too.'

'Oh, I'm sure it is. But I feel certain you'll give it to me nevertheless. Won't you, Walter?'

'Why should I? I owe it to my client to respect his wish to remain anonymous.'

Grant laughed derisively. 'Ah, come off it. Don't you try pulling that one too. You aren't telling me you were simply acting as an agent for somebody, are you? That isn't the way you work. You're a dealer; you buy things and you sell things. So now I'm going to re-phrase my question. Who did you buy it from?'

'Go to hell,' Munnet said.

'Eventually perhaps. But not before I've been to the boys in blue and invited them to have a look into the matter. I'd say they might be interested, wouldn't you?'

Munnet looked at him uneasily. 'You wouldn't do that.'

'Why not?'

'What good would it do you?'

'They might get the information I'm asking for. They can exert a lot more pressure than I can. Do you want them poking into your business affairs, examining the books and all that?'

'They do enough of that already.' Munnet spoke sulkily. 'Bastards!'

'Yes, I expect they do. That's because they've got you down as a character who can bear watching. But if I were to tell them what I know about *Bavarian Sunset* they might have something juicy to get their teeth into.'

'What do you know?'

'That the item came into your possession in suspicious circumstances. With similar items perhaps.'

'You don't know that. You're just guessing.'

'Maybe so. But they'd be bound to follow up a lead coming from me. So wouldn't it be much easier for you just to give me the name and leave the police out of it?'

Munnet was silent for a while. He was obviously debating in his mind the relative desirability of the alternatives open to him. Grant was convinced that he would not wish to have the police involved, and it was the threat of this possibility that must have turned the scale in the end.

'All right,' he said, 'I'll tell you if you'll give me your word you won't go to the coppers.'

'Trust me for that,' Grant assured him. 'You play fair with me and I'll play fair with you. Now let's have the name.'

'Lennie Peck.'

'Well, well, well! So that's who you got the picture from. Now I can understand why you wanted to keep it a secret and not have the officers of the law making inquiries. One sniff of Lennie and they'd be swarming round here, like wasps on a rotten plum. It was very naughty of you to have dealings with a character like him.'

'Never mind that.' Munnet spoke testily. 'I don't need any lectures from you on how to run my business.'

'And I'm not going to give any, because I know it wouldn't do a bit of good. You're set in your nasty little ways and you're too old to change them now. But you really were taking a risk, weren't you? Did Lennie tell you how he came by the picture?'

'He said he bought it in France when he was on holiday.'

'He was joking, of course. You knew he was.'

'I didn't know. He could've been telling the truth.'

'For the first time in his life. Don't try to play the little innocent with me, Walter; it doesn't suit you. Anything that Lennie Peck has to offer for sale is bound to have been acquired by dishonest means. He's a tea-leaf and you know it.'

'If you say so.' Munnet had lapsed into a grumpy mood. 'You're the clever one. You know all the answers.'

'No, Walter, not all of them. For instance, I don't know where Lennie is living these days. I haven't seen him lately.'

'So you want me to tell you that too?'

'If you don't mind.'

'I do mind. I mind a great deal. But I don't suppose it'll make the least bit of difference. You've still got too much of the policeman in you, Mr Grant, and that's straight. You should've stayed in the Force.'

'So I've been told. But I didn't and that's that. So now the address, please.'

Munnet, with a very bad grace, gave it to him, and he wrote it down.

* * *

Lennie Peck was living with a girlfriend named Shirley in a mobile home on a piece of waste ground in the Stepney area of East London. Shirley was no bimbo; she was in fact rather mature for a girlfriend and might have been more accurately described as a lady-friend if she had been anything of a lady, which she was not. She was a faded blonde, running to fat; but the mobile home was hers; which was possibly why Lennie Peck stuck with her. It gave him somewhere to get his feet under the table when he was not being accommodated in one of the nation's free hotels; the kind with high walls and barbed wire round them.

Not that Peck himself was any woman's dream of a Prince Charming. He was a little runt of a man, not much bigger than Walter Munnet, getting on towards his fiftieth year, with narrow shoulders and a face like a wrinkled cherub. Grant's acquaintanceship with him went back as far as that with the antiques dealer, and it too was professional rather than social.

He drove out to Stepney in the early evening in his car, a not very new Ford Escort, which he had recently acquired to replace an even less new Maestro. He had had some trouble with the Escort and he suspected he might have been sold a pup, but it was too late now to ask for his money back. It had to be marked up to experience.

There were some other mobile homes on the site, and none of them looked very smart; indeed, there was a depressed and dilapidated appearance about the whole place, and the buildings surrounding it did nothing to improve matters; they were just as dingy themselves.

It was the woman who opened the door in answer to Grant's knock; and he was not surprised to see her because Munnet had told him about her in not very complimentary terms. There were a couple of brick steps leading up to the door, and she stood looking down at him from her superior position with no great evidence of being at all pleased with what she was seeing.

'Yes?'

'I'm looking for a man named Peck,' Grant said. 'Lennie Peck. I was told he lived here.'

'What you want with him?'

'A word or two. My name is Grant. He knows me.'

'Oh, he does, does he? What are you? A copper?'

It was curious, Grant thought, that she should have jumped to that immediate conclusion. But understandable perhaps, since she must have had a pretty good knowledge of Peck's dubious activities.

'No, I'm not a copper. Is Mr Peck at home?'

She seemed half-inclined to give a negative answer to the question, but at that moment Peck appeared behind her, head craning to get a sight of the caller. He showed no more pleasure at what he saw than the woman had, though he did make some attempt to sound affable.

'Why, Mr Grant. Is that you?'

'Who does it look like?' Grant asked. 'How are you these days, Lennie?'

'So so. You keepin' well?'

Grant felt quite sure that Peck was no more concerned about his health than he was with Peck's, so he ignored the question and suggested that he should be allowed to step inside.

'There's a little matter I'd like to discuss with you, if you can spare the time.'

'Or even if I can't, I s'pose,' Peck said, feebly jocular. 'Well, step aside, Shirl, and let the man come in.'

She did so with some apparent reluctance, eyeing Grant with a mixture of distaste and suspicion as he stepped up into the home. She closed the door and stood with her back to it, arms akimbo, watching the visitor distrustfully.

'Nice place you have here,' Grant said. It was a lie; there was nothing nice about it; it was shoddy and the furnishing had a much-used look about it. 'Cosy.'

'It's a bloody dump,' the woman said. 'And you know it.'

Peck gave an embarrassed grin and invited Grant to sit down. He did so on a settee which was a built-in feature on one side of what might have been described as the living-room. Peck also sat down, but the woman remained standing, hostility only too evident in her whole attitude.

'Look, Shirl,' Peck said, 'why don't you get a can of beer for our guest?'

'No beer, thanks,' Grant said. 'I've got my car and I don't drink and drive.'

'Sensible man. Too much of it around. But you'll have something? Coffee? Make some coffee, Shirl. I'll have a cup too; I feel a bit thirsty.'

Grant thought for a moment she was going to refuse, but then she gave a toss of the head and a sniff and went into what was evidently a kitchen at one end of the accommodation. She could be heard in there venting some of her bad temper on the mugs and spoons.

'Bottled gas,' Peck said.

'Come again?'

'Bottled gas. It's what we use for cooking.'

'Oh, yes, I see.'

'Long time since I seen you last,' Peck said. He seemed to be doing his best to keep the conversation going on innocuous subjects, as if to delay the broaching of the true purpose of Grant's visit. He was fidgety, unable to disguise his nervousness. 'How many years ago was it?'

'Quite a few. There was a little matter of some stolen property you were able to give me some information about.'

'Oh, was I? I'd forgotten.'

'Like hell you had! Saved your own skin that time. Maybe you've got the chance to save it again in much the same way.'

'Dunno wotcher mean,' Peck said. 'What're you getting at?'

Before Grant could answer Shirley came back with two mugs of coffee and interrupted the conversation. She set the mugs down on a table as if she could not bring herself to do more than that in the way of service, and left them to help themselves. Peck stood up and handed one of the mugs to Grant, taking the other for himself.

Grant took a sip of the coffee, which was sweet and strong. He looked at Peck.

'You want to know what I'm getting at, Lennie?' He glanced at the woman. 'It's rather a private matter.'

The woman spoke sharply. 'Anything you've got to say to him, you can say in my hearing. Any business of his is my business too. We don't have no secrets from each other. Ain't that so, Lennie?'

She was still standing and she had made no coffee for herself. She seemed determined not to show any hint of friendliness. Grant had the impression that she was a tough customer, and he was glad that he was not dealing with her rather than Lennie, who was probably a lot more malleable. Munnet had hinted that in her younger days she had made her living on the streets, and in that trade it was as well to be tough. Maybe she did a bit in that line even now, though she had rather run to seed.

Peck gave a wriggle of the shoulders, which might have been taken as an acceptance of what she had said. Certainly he was not denying it.

'Okay then,' Grant said, 'I'll tell you. I'm getting at a piece of business concerning a picture entered in an auction by a Mr Walter Munnet, a dealer in antiques. Does that ring any sort of bell in this household?'

The woman said nothing. She just stared at Grant, stony-faced. Peck licked his lips and said:

'What picture?'

'One called *Bavarian Sunset* by Arnold Sempler. As if you hadn't guessed.'

Peck had a hunted look. 'What would that have to do

with me?'

'Quite a lot, I should say. Seeing that Munnet had the article in question from you.'

'He told you that?'

'After some hesitation. I had to apply a bit of pressure to get him to cough up.'

'Pressure?'

'Like threatening to go to the police.'

'And then he told you he had the picture off of me?'

'Yes.'

'He was lying. I never sold him no picture. I never had nothing to do with pictures, straight I never.'

Grant shook his head. 'You're the one who's lying. He was telling the truth. Think about it. Why would he pluck your name out of the air like that if it wasn't the right one?'

'I dunno. Maybe he's got it in for me.'

'You'll have to think of something better than that, Lennie. It just won't wash.'

'Lay off him,' Shirley said. 'What right have you to come in here accusing people of stealing valuable pictures?'

'Who said it was stolen? I didn't.'

'It's what you was incinerating.'

'Was I? Well anyway, whether it was stolen or not isn't the point just now. I simply want some information about it.'

'What sort of information?'

'Like where it came from. Like who had it before it fell into Lennie's sticky little paw. That kind of thing.'

Peck burst out suddenly, his voice petulant: 'He shouldn't have told you. He give me his word he wouldn't tell no one. I'll kill the old bastard, see if I don't.'

'No you won't, Lennie,' Grant said. He was pleased to see that Peck was no longer attempting to deny that he had supplied Munnet with the painting. It was a pretence that could hardly have been maintained, and he must have realised it. 'Killing isn't in your line, you know. Thieving, yes, but killing, no. You wouldn't have the nerve for that. And besides, there's no harm done. All I want to know is where you got the picture.'

Peck answered sullenly: 'I bought it.'

'Oh, yes, I know. In France when you were on holiday. That's what you told Walter. He didn't believe it and I don't believe it either.'

'Well, you can please yourself about that.'

'You mean that's your story and you're sticking to it?'

'Yes.'

'Now you're being stubborn. And not very clever. It won't work. I told you I had to put pressure on Walter. Now I see I shall have to put some on you as well.'

'Howja mean?'

'I could go to the police, tell them what I know. It would be enough to bring them round here for an interview. And that wouldn't be too nice for you, would it? You could end up inside again, and at your age it would come hard. I don't really think you'd want that, would you?'

In an agony of indecision Peck cast an imploring glance at the woman, as if seeking help from her in his predicament. It was not in vain. She spoke to Grant, sounding less antagonistic than before.

'Suppose he was to tell you what you want to know. Would that be enough? You'd give your word not to go to the coppers?'

'Yes. I'm not aiming to get Lennie into trouble as long as he's co-operative.'

'But how do we know we can trust you to keep to your side of the bargain?'

'You don't. But what option have you got? Anyway, as I said, I'm not interested in putting Lennie away. I'm a private investigator; I only do what I'm paid to do. And I'm not being paid to put the finger on him. He's just incidental.'

Shirley gave him a closer look and spoke disdainfully. 'A private eye! I might have guessed. So who are you working for?'

'Now, now,' Grant said. 'You wouldn't really expect me to tell you that, would you?'

'Why not? You're asking Lennie to confide in you.'

'That's different. He's in no position to refuse. Are you, Lennie? Don't want a copper to come feeling your collar again, do you?'

'All right,' Peck said grumpily. 'You've got me over a barrel. I did steal that there picture.'

'Now you're being sensible and we're getting to the truth of it. Like to tell me when and where, and who it was you stole it from?'

'I don't know the geezer's name.'

'Oh, come, Lennie, you'll have to do better than that. You rob somebody of a picture and you don't know who he is?'

'It's God's truth. Me and Shirley, we was out for a drive in the country and I happened to see this big house which seemed a likely place for a job, so I made a note of it and went back later.'

'Just like that? Without even finding out who the owner of the property was?'

'Yes.'

'Is that your system? To go around in your car looking for likely targets for your nefarious operations?'

'I wouldn't call it that azackly; not a system. It's just the way I work sometimes.'

It was not a very professional way, in Grant's opinion; but Lennie Peck was not much of a professional. He was an opportunist who took advantage of other people's carelessness. He was a loner, too; he never worked with a gang; perhaps because no self-respecting gang would have him. He was certainly none too bright; that was probably why he had been put away quite a few times.

'So you're telling me you pinched a valuable painting from someone whose name you don't know and whom you've never seen?'

'Oh, I seen him. Leastways, I reckon it was him. It was like this here, see: I got in through a French window what'd been left unlocked, though it was well arter midnight and there wasn't no lights on in the house, and I found myself in this big room with a lot of pictures on the walls. I was shining my torch on them and wondering whether to take some and leave pretty damn quick or go round hunting for the family silver and suchlike, which would be easier to carry and maybe more saleable anyway, when I heard a door open behind me and the click of the light switch. I swung round and there was this old bald-headed geezer in a dressing-gown and slippers staring at me with his eyes nearly popping out of his head, like he'd seen a ghost or something.

'He didn't say nothing, just stood staring, petrified like, with his mouth open, and I reckon he was as scared as what I was. I didn't really think what I was doing; it was just instinct, I reckon; self-preservation, as you might say. He didn't have nothing in his hands, no weapon nor anything like that. He hadn't been expecting to find anyone in the room, I s'pose. Anyway,

I just took three or four steps and hit him with the torch on the side of the noggin. He gave a sort of squeak, not at all loud, not much more than the sound a mouse would make, and he bent at the knees and went down.

'I didn't wait to see if he would get up again; I just made tracks. But I didn't like to leave with nothing; I meanter say it would've been a waste of effort, wouldn't it? Still, there was no sense in hanging around, picking and choosing, because there was no telling when the old geezer might perk up and start yelling bloody murder. So I took the first thing that came to hand, and it happened to be that there picture. It was hanging within easy reach and it wasn't too big, so I grabbed it and scarpered.

'I went like a bat outa hell down the drive, expecting any moment to hear somebody giving chase. But there wasn't nobody and there was a fair bit of moonlight to show me the way, so I didn't need to use the torch. At the end of the drive was some iron gates but they wasn't closed, and I got meself out on to the road and ran another hundred yards or so to where I'd left my car on the verge under some trees.

'I bunged the picture in the boot and got in and drove off, and that was that. No more trouble. No trouble at all until you turned up and started asking questions.'

'So that's the whole story?' Grant said.

'That's it.' Lennie Peck took a drink from the cup of coffee, which was getting cold. He fumbled in his pocket and brought out a squashed packet of cigarettes, one of which he lighted, his hand shaking a little, as though he were suffering again from the shock of being discovered in the act of committing a felony.

'I hope you're satisfied now, Mr Private Eye,' Shirley said. 'You've got all you're going to get out of him.'

'But not the name of the owner of the picture. The man in the dressing-gown. If it was him.'

'Well, that's just too bad. You'll have to make do with what you've got. He can't tell you no more.'

'Oh, I'm not so sure. How about the name of the house, Lennie?'

'I don't know it.'

'Do you mean to say there was no sign or anything at the entrance?'

'Not that I noticed.'

Grant turned to Shirley. 'Did you see anything?'

'No, I never see a thing.' She seemed quite pleased to be able to deny any knowledge of the name of the house, and probably would not have told him even if she had been able to. It was quite apparent that she had taken an instant dislike to him, and the revelation that he was a private investigator had only served to intensify the ill-feeling. 'So now you'd better go. There's nothing more for you here.'

Grant answered coolly: 'Maybe there is. I imagine you could still find the place, couldn't you, Lennie?'

Peck answered reluctantly: 'I reckon so.'

'Then tomorrow you and I will take a trip out there. It'll be a nice little outing for you. You'll enjoy it.'

'Oh, gawd!' Lennie said.

FOUR

For a Client

They went in Grant's car with Peck as navigator. The place was in Hertfordshire, on the outskirts of a village called Maddenhall Superior. There was a Maddenhall Inferior too, but that was five miles away, and Grant wondered whether its inhabitants ever suffered from an inferiority complex.

Not that there was anything obviously superior about the other Maddenhall; it comprised a rather scattered collection of houses of various ages, some thatched, with a village green and a pond in the centre and a few clumps of trees here and there. It looked peaceful and rather picturesque. There was a church with a square tower, one public-house and a general shop which served also as a post-office. There were ducks swimming on the pond.

'Nice little place,' Grant remarked.

'You can keep it,' Peck said. He was not in the mood to appreciate the attractions of a country village.

The house they were looking for was half a mile or so further on. It stood well back from the road and was partly obscured by trees. It was certainly not a mansion, but it was fairly large; a four-square building which could have been the home of a well-to-do country gentleman, if such people still existed.

Grant had stopped the car outside the iron gates at the end of the drive and was taking a good look at the house.

'So that's the place.'

'Yes, that's the place,' Peck said. 'And if you're thinking of paying a call on the owner you can count me out.' He seemed edgy, possibly fearing that the man he had assaulted and robbed might suddenly appear and recognise him.

Grant gave some thought to the suggestion that he might go up to the house and meet the owner, but decided on reflection that the time had not yet come for that. Instead he turned the car and drove back to the village; a move which seemed to puzzle Lennie Peck.

'Is that the lot?'

'Not quite,' Grant said. 'I'm going to make some inquiries and I think I know a likely place for it.'

He stopped the car outside the shop which doubled as a post-office, and telling Peck to remain where he was, he got out and made his way to the shop door. Entering, he discovered that the postal counter was just inside on the left, caged off from the rest of the store where the groceries and other goods were displayed.

Three or four women with shopping-bags made the rather limited floor area seem crowded, and it was apparent that they knew one another and were taking the opportunity to exchange a few items of gossip as they did their shopping. A girl of about eighteen in a green overall was attending to them, and there was a middle-aged woman behind the grille of the postal section who was weighing a parcel that a tow-haired boy had brought in. When she had dealt with him Grant bought a book of stamps for the look of the thing and then made his inquiries.

'I wonder if you could help me,' he said. 'As I was driving towards the village I happened to see on my left a large house standing in its own grounds. There were tall wrought-iron gates hanging on stone pillars at the end of the drive. Do you know the place I'm referring to?'

'Oh,' she said, 'that'll be Marley Hall, I expect.'

'Marley Hall, eh? I suppose it wouldn't be a Mr Hagen living there, would it? An old friend I've lost touch with for years. I believe he has a place somewhere around here.'

'Oh no, sir; I'm afraid you won't find your friend up there.' She seemed quite regretful at having to disappoint him. 'It's Mr Reedham that has the hall. It's been in the family for generations. Won't be any more though after Mr Clifford is gone, him being a bachelor with no one to leave it to.'

'Mr Clifford Reedham. No, that's certainly not my man.'

The woman lowered her voice to a conspiratorial level. 'Just as well really. Bit of a black sheep of the family by all accounts.'

'Is that so? Well, I suppose most families have them. Thanks for your help anyway.'

'You're welcome,' she said. 'Sorry I couldn't be more help with your Mr Hagen.'

Grant left the shop and rejoined Peck in the car.

'Find out what you wanted to know?' Peck asked.

'Yes.'

'Are you going to tell me, or is it a secret?'

Grant started the car and put it on course for a return to London. 'I see no reason why I should tell you,

Lennie. If you wanted to know the man's name you should have asked him when you had the chance instead of hitting him on the bean with a torch.'

'Oh, very funny,' Peck said. After which he sank into a moody silence which lasted for most of the journey back to London.

Grant dropped him off at his rather depressing abode and went to get himself a meal.

* * *

'His name,' Grant said, 'is Clifford Reedham and he's living at a place called Marley Hall in Hertfordshire.'

Gerda Hoffmann digested this piece of information and then said: 'So what you are telling me is that this man Reedham used the antiques dealer as an agent to enter the painting in the auction?'

Grant shook his head. 'No, that is not what I am telling you. The painting was sold to the dealer by a thief, our man Walter Munnet being something of a fence on the side.'

'A fence?'

'Receiver of stolen property.'

'Oh, I see. And it was this thief who stole it from Mr Reedham, was it?'

'That's it.'

'How did you manage to discover all this? I mean the dealer and the thief wouldn't be very happy about giving away information that was likely to incriminate them, would they?'

'You're dead right, they wouldn't.'

'So?'

'So I had to persuade them.'

'I see.'

'He can be very persuasive when he puts his mind to it,' Cynara remarked. 'He leans on people, you know.'

The three of them were again in the office of the Samuel Grant Inquiry Agency in Shepherd's Bush, which was where they had arranged to meet for a progress report. You had to climb a flight of bare wooden stairs to get to it and the name was on the door; which was a help to prospective clients who might otherwise have found themselves in the clutches of the photographer on one side or the seedy tax-consultant on the other. Since leaving the employ of Mr Alexander Peking and setting up on his own account Grant had had his ups and downs, but rather too many of the latter. He now had a displayed advertisement in the Yellow Pages, but he was not sure it was earning what it cost to keep it there. Sometimes he had a feeling that he was in the wrong line of business, but what was the alternative? He was not qualified for any other kind of job and times were hard.

'Did you see Mr Reedham?' Gerda asked.

'No. I didn't think it was necessary at this stage. All you asked me to do was to find out his name.'

'That's true. And you feel quite sure he is the man I'm looking for?'

'Well,' Grant said, 'let's put it this way: I'm sure he's the one who had the painting until it was stolen. But I've no knowledge of whoever may have owned it before him. It may have been in his possession for years or he could have acquired it quite recently.'

'Yes, I suppose that is so,' Miss Hoffmann admitted; and it seemed to depress her a little.

'You still don't feel like telling me why you want to find this person? It might help, you know.'

But apparently she was not ready for that yet. 'Don't

be so impatient. And I don't see how it could help at all, except to satisfy your curiosity.'

'And mine too,' Cynara said. 'I'm dying to know what this is all about. It's very intriguing.'

Gerda smiled. 'Perhaps it is. But you also will have to be patient for a while.'

'So what now?' Grant asked. 'Do you need my services any longer or is this where I bow out?'

'Of course it isn't. I still need you very much. We have to make sure whether or not this Mr Reedham is the one I'm looking for.'

'And how do we do that?'

'Well,' she said, 'it seems to me that there is only one way of doing that. We must go and see him.'

'And just by seeing him you'll know?'

'Well, no, not quite. It will be necessary to ask a few questions, of course.'

'Such as?'

'Such as where did he get the picture; how long had he had it and so on.'

'Suppose he doesn't wish to answer any questions? What then? There's no reason why he should, you know. He may even refuse to see us.'

'Then you must persuade him.' She gave a charming smile. 'And we all know how good you are at persuasion, don't we?'

Grant resisted the charm. 'I need something to work on if I'm to ring Reedham up and ask for an appointment. I shall have to give him a good reason for wanting to see him.'

'So tell him you have a client who is interested in the work of Arnold Sempler and you believe he has a Sempler painting.'

'But he hasn't. It was stolen. Remember?'

'Never mind. I have a feeling he'll be curious to know why someone should be looking for Arnold Semplers just after he's had one stolen from him. Don't you think so?'

Grant stared at her, trying to read her mind. He felt certain there was more to it than that. And of course it all had to do with the true reason for her search; the reason she was still withholding from him. But once again it boiled down to the one basic fact that she was the client and he either had to carry out her instructions or withdraw his services. And as long as she was prepared to pay him he had no wish to withdraw. Besides which, like Cynara, he was intrigued. There was a mystery here and he wanted to get to the bottom of it.

'All right then,' he said. 'I'll try to make that appointment. Don't count on anything, though. For all we know he may be a recluse who puts a high value on his privacy.'

'Oh,' she said, smiling sweetly at him again, 'I feel sure you will manage to bring him round. I have absolute confidence in you. You are such a capable person, are you not?'

It was blatant flattery of course, and he knew it. But he was no more immune to flattery than the next man; nor to the charms of a woman as attractive as Miss Hoffmann undoubtedly was.

'Well, I'll try. But as I said, don't expect too much. That way you won't be disappointed.'

This time she just smiled.

* * *

'My name is Grant,' he said. 'I am acting on behalf of a client who would very much like to have an interview with you if that is in any way possible.'

He had found the telephone number by consulting Directory Enquiries, and then he had put a call through to Marley Hall. It was Mr Clifford Reedham himself who answered the telephone.

'An interview!' Reedham's voice sounded somewhat querulous. 'What is this? Some kind of joke?'

'Not at all. I –'

'You're selling something. That's it, isn't it? Well, I can tell you straightaway I'm not interested. If it's double-glazing or a fitted kitchen or any other damned thing, I don't want it. Got that?'

'I've got it,' Grant said. 'But I'm not selling anything. As I said, all I want is to arrange an interview with you for a third person.'

'Nonsense. Why on earth would anyone want to interview me? I'm not famous. I'm not a pop star or a professional footballer. I'm just an old man who would like to be left in peace.'

'I appreciate that, Mr Reedham, but this would take very little time and my client is very anxious to meet you. It would be a great disappointment for her if you were to refuse.'

'Her! So it's a woman?'

'Yes.'

'Now what the devil would any woman want with me?'

'Just a few words.'

'On what subject, for God's sake?'

'Let's say art.'

'Art! Now I know you're crazy. What do you take me for? An artist?'

'I don't know what you are, Mr Reedham. I am merely a go-between trying to arrange a meeting.'

'Then you're wasting your time. I'm not seeing anyone, and that's that. Tell your client she'll have to find someone else to talk to about art, because I'm not interested.'

In another moment Grant felt certain the man would slam down the receiver, so he spoke quickly.

'It's not art in general she wishes to speak to you about. There's one particular artist she's concerned with; a man named Arnold Sempler, who died in a Nazi concentration camp during World War Two.'

There was silence on the line; not because Reedham had put the receiver down but because for the moment he was saying nothing. Grant felt pretty certain that the name of Sempler had touched a nerve and had stopped Reedham in his tracks.

He waited. The seconds ticked by. When Reedham spoke again the querulous note had gone from his voice and he seemed to be choosing his words with care.

'Did you say Arnold Sempler?'

'Yes. You have heard of him, I daresay?'

'Yes, I have heard of him.'

'I rather thought you would have.'

'This client of yours,' Reedham said. 'What is her name?'

'Gerda Hoffmann.'

'Hoffmann! That is a German name, is it not?'

'Yes. Miss Hoffmann is German.'

'Ah!'

Again there was silence. Again Grant had the feeling that he had given Reedham food for thought. He himself was working rather in the dark because he had been told so little by his client, but he could tell that his words were having an impact on the man at the other end of the line.

Reedham asked another question: 'Why should Miss Hoffmann wish to talk to me about this Arnold

Sempler?'

'Because she believes you are the owner of a work of his: a painting called *Bavarian Sunset*.'

'Ah!' Again that brief exclamation. Surprise perhaps? Or possibly concern? Hard to tell.

It was interesting, Grant reflected, that Reedham had made no denial that he had such a painting. He did not say that it had been stolen and was no longer in his possession. It was odd, that.

'Very well,' Reedham said at last. 'I will talk to Miss Hoffmann.'

'Good. When would be a convenient day and time for me to bring her to meet you?'

There followed another pause. Then: 'Tomorrow morning. Eleven o'clock. Might as well get it over with, I suppose.' He spoke as if referring to some unpleasant task that had to be performed. 'You can manage that?'

'I think so. If not I'll be in touch.'

*   *   *

'You did that rather well,' Gerda said. She and Cynara had remained in the office while Grant did the telephoning. 'I take it he agreed to a meeting?'

'Yes. Tomorrow at eleven a.m. at his place.'

'That's fine. Couldn't be better. And you're going to take me there, are you?'

'If that's what you want.'

'It is.'

'Then it's no problem. But there are one or two things I find rather puzzling.'

'Yes?' Eyebrows lifting slightly in question.

'Well, in the first place he wasn't at all willing to agree to the meeting, and I think he was on the point of ringing off. But when I mentioned Arnold Sempler I could almost see his ears pricking up, and after that he was really interested. Shaken too, I'd say; especially when I told him your name and that you were German. It certainly appeared to get through to him somehow. Have you any idea why that should have been so?'

'Perhaps.'

'But you're not telling?'

'I think not.'

'As you please. But there was something else that was pretty odd. He didn't deny that he owned *Bavarian Sunset*, but he made no mention of the fact that it had been stolen. Doesn't that seem a trifle strange to you?'

She did not give a direct answer to the question; she merely said: 'Perhaps he was just being cautious. After all, he doesn't know you, does he?'

'That's true. But I wouldn't be surprised if he's guessed I'm a private investigator, although I didn't actually tell him that.'

Cynara threw her contribution into the discussion then. 'Well anyway,' she said, 'we should find out the answers to some of our questions when we see him tomorrow.'

Grant looked at her. 'We? Who said you were going?'

'But of course I am. I'm interested too, you know.' She turned to Gerda. 'You don't have any objection, do you?'

'None at all,' Miss Hoffmann said.

'Mr Reedham may have. He'll be expecting two people, not three.'

'Stuff Mr Reedham,' Cynara said. Which was crude but emphatic.

Grant raised no further objection; he accepted the fact that there would be three of them going down to Marley Hall.

FIVE

From the Past

They started in good time, to allow for any delays there might be on the way. Grant had picked Gerda up at her hotel and she was beside him in the passenger seat. Cynara was riding in the back.

It was a pleasant morning and Gerda was obviously enjoying the outing, especially after they had left the sprawl of London behind and were in the Hertfordshire countryside. She talked animatedly and seemed to be in the best of spirits. Grant guessed that she had already jumped to the conclusion that Reedham was the man she had been looking for, and he thought it wise to sound a note of caution.

'This could lead to a dead end, you know. Reedham may not be your man.'

But she refused to be discouraged. 'I have a feeling that he is. Call it intuition if you like.'

'I'm not sure I do.' Grant spoke drily. There was something called woman's intuition, but he did not put much faith in it. Cynara claimed to have it, but he had never found any solid evidence for the accuracy of her intuitions. He could have managed as well with blind guessing.

Gerda was enchanted by the village of Maddenhall Superior. 'It's so quaint; like something out of a picture-book. It looks as if it hasn't changed in centuries. It must have looked just like this ages ago.'

'If you ignore the telephone and electricity wires and the TV aerials and dishes,' Grant said. 'Not to mention the double-decker bus picking up some passengers.'

'Don't be so cynical,' Cynara admonished him. 'You know it looks nice anyway.'

But there was little time to dwell on the niceness of Maddenhall Superior, because they were not stopping there and a few minutes later they had reached the gateway that gave access to the drive leading up to Marley Hall.

The immediate impression Grant had from the outside was of a certain neglect, of a place being allowed to fall into a gradual decline. The grounds were unkempt; there were areas of rough grass and weeds where trim lawns might once have been; shrubs had become straggly and overgrown, and the gravel of the drive was weedy. The exterior of the hall, which had looked well enough from the road, was revealed on closer inspection to be suffering from dilapidation; nothing really bad as yet, but a leaking gutter here and there, a suggestion of wet rot in the window-frames and some peeling and blistered paint. Virginia creeper on the walls had been allowed to grow rampantly and was getting out of hand. Neglect was apparent everywhere.

Grant stopped the car in front of a porch supported by stone pillars and they all got out. A tug on a rusty iron bell-pull brought a man to the door, who stared at them with undisguised hostility. He was old but not decayed. Though slightly stooping, he was powerfully built, with broad shoulders and a thick neck, his face

deeply creased and with a weathered look about it; his
hair white but plentiful, cropped short and standing up
stiffly, rather like the bristles of a scrubbing-brush. His
voice was harsh and unfriendly.

'Yes?'

'We have an appointment with Mr Reedham,' Grant
said. It was easy to guess that this was not Reedham
himself but a servant, though he was hardly dressed like
one, having on a pair of baggy corduroy trousers, a
collarless shirt and a woollen cardigan, wearing out at
the elbows.

'You'll be Mr Grant then?'

'Yes.'

The man in the cardigan stared at him, his eyes
overhung by bushy eyebrows that were almost as white
as his hair. Then he glanced at the women.

'He said there'd be just the two of you.'

'So there's one extra. Does it matter?'

'Not to me, it don't. He may not like it, though.'

'So why don't you just tell him we're here and leave it
to him to decide?'

The man decided to accept this suggestion and
gruffly invited them to step into the entrance hall, a
chilly area of tiled floor with minimal furnishing.

'Wait here.'

He walked with a lumbering gait to a door on the
right, opened it without knocking and went into the
room to which it gave access. They could hear a low
murmur of voices, and then the man in the cardigan
reappeared and said: 'All right. He'll see you.'

He remained by the door and shepherded them into
the room where Reedham was seated in an armchair.
This room was only slightly less chilly than the hall,
although a log fire was burning in a large open

fireplace. Most of the heat was evidently escaping by way of a cavernous chimney, blackened by soot. The room itself was large, with a high smoke-stained ceiling, from which hung a chandelier. The furniture was old but solid, the upholstery of armchairs and sofa matching in its way the exterior dilapidation. There were cobwebs and dust in abundance, as though no one had wielded a broom or a duster in there for some considerable time.

Reedham stood up when they entered. He appeared to be somewhat younger than the manservant, possibly seventy or so; but he was far less robust. He was tall and thin, though there was still a certain chubbiness about his face; the nose inclined to the snub, mouth oddly small and pouting, incongruously like a child's. His hair, which was confined now to the lower slopes of his head at the back and sides, was of a faded gingery colour, and all his skin was sprinkled with freckles. On his left temple was a small scar which might have been the legacy of a recent blow.

He made a somewhat languid gesture with his hand, indicating chairs and sofa. 'Please sit down.' He made no offer to shake hands with the visitors, and when they had seated themselves he went back to his own chair.

The manservant was still hovering in the doorway, and he dismissed him. 'That will be all, Cragg. You may go now.' He spoke with a cultured accent and he was dressed in the style of a country gentleman: Harris tweed suit and stout walking shoes.

Cragg did not leave instantly; he seemed inclined to stay and lend an ear if not a voice to the conversation; but Reedham made a pettish gesture of dismissal and he departed, though with some apparent reluctance, closing the door behind him with rather more energy than was strictly necessary, as though registering his displeasure at being thus banished.

Reedham made a kind of apology for the manners of his servant. 'A rough diamond, Cragg, but indispensable, quite indispensable. It's so difficult to get reliable domestic staff these days. Staff of any kind for that matter.'

'Is he your only servant?' Grant asked.

'For the present, yes, unfortunately,' Reedham admitted. Then, turning to the women: 'Which of you ladies is Miss Hoffmann?'

'I am,' Gerda said.

'Ah!' He gave her an appraising look, his gaze resting on her face for a few moments as though he were trying to read something there. Then it moved on to Cynara. 'And you are?'

'Miss Jones. I am a friend of Miss Hoffmann's. I asked if I might come along. For the ride. I hope you don't mind.'

'I? Why should I mind? It makes no difference to me who comes.' It was not a particularly gracious remark; he spoke a trifle sarcastically, not bothering to hide the fact that he would have preferred to have none of them there and was only tolerating their presence on sufferance.

Grant had the impression that Reedham was nervous, though he was doing his best to appear at ease. One thing was certain: he was anxious to learn what Miss Hoffmann's interest in the Sempler painting might be, and it was he who broached the subject.

'So then, let's get down to business, shall we? I understand, Miss Hoffmann, that you are interested in a certain work of art which you believe I own.'

'*Bavarian Sunset* by Arnold Sempler, yes. I should

very much like to examine it.'

'Ah!' Reedham said. 'Now that could present quite a bit of a problem.'

'Really? Why?'

'Because it is no longer in my possession.'

'You have sold it?'

'Well, no, not exactly sold.'

"What then?'

'It has been stolen.'

Miss Hoffmann gave a passable impression of being surprised to hear this. 'Stolen!'

'Yes. One night I heard a sound in one of the rooms. I went into it to investigate and was immediately attacked by an intruder. He struck me on the head with some kind of bludgeon and knocked me out.' Reedham touched the scar with a finger. 'As you see, I still have the mark. When I came to the intruder had gone and so had *Bavarian Sunset.*'

'How unfortunate.'

'Unfortunate indeed. And the direct result of my own carelessness. I had omitted to lock the French windows; made it easy for the thief.'

'So you don't have a burglar alarm?' Grant said.

'No. I've never bothered with anything of that sort.'

'Maybe you should have done. But I expect the police told you as much.'

'Police! What police?'

'Why, those you reported the robbery to. You did report it, I suppose?'

Reedham showed some embarrassment. 'Well, no; as a matter of fact I didn't.'

'Why on earth not?'

'I didn't think it worth the bother.'

'Not worth the bother when you had been assaulted

and had a valuable painting stolen?'

'What good would it have done? How often do the police catch the criminal? They crawl all over you, asking questions, making a damned nuisance of themselves, and in the end what happens? It goes on file as another unsolved crime.'

'But the painting –'

'Oh, that! Well, it was of no great value anyway.'

Miss Hoffmann took the liberty of disagreeing. 'That is not true. There has been increasing interest in the works of Arnold Sempler in recent years. The number of paintings by him is limited and the value has risen.'

'Is that so? I had no idea. Well, well, well!'

Grant did not believe that Reedham's surprise was genuine; he would have made a bet that the man was lying.

'Had you had the painting long?' Gerda asked.

'Quite a while. Oh yes, quite a considerable while.'

'You bought it in Germany, perhaps?'

'Oh, good lord, no. Came across it in a junk shop in Bournemouth – or it may have been Brighton – can't remember for certain. Little place selling antiques and that sort of thing. Liked the look of it and as it was going for a song I bought it.'

He's lying again, Grant thought. He was watching Reedham closely. The man's gaze was on Miss Hoffmann's face; it might have been that he was observing her reaction to his words; trying to tell whether she believed his story. But as far as Grant could see she was giving no clue to her thoughts.

'I suppose you wouldn't be able to tell me the name of the shop?' she asked.

'Sorry, no. As I said, so long ago.'

'And you haven't got the receipt?'

'After all these years! Hardly. But why do you wish to know?'

'I was thinking that the people in the shop might have been able to help me. You see I'm trying to get in touch with the previous owner. What I would really like to know is how the painting came to this country from Germany.'

'I see,' Reedham said; and he seemed to think about this. Then: 'Any particular reason?'

'Just research. I'm planning to write a book on the life and works of Arnold Sempler and I need to have as much information on the subject as I can possibly get.'

Reedham nodded. 'I understand.' And Grant felt sure he did not believe a word of what Miss Hoffmann had said. For that matter, neither did he.

Suddenly Miss Hoffmann asked a personal question. 'Were you in the British army during the last war, Mr Reedham?'

He seemed startled for a moment, but quickly regained his composure. 'Yes, I was as a matter of fact.'

'Perhaps you took part in the liberation of Europe towards the end of the conflict?'

He looked at her warily, as though trying to figure out where she was leading him. 'Yes, I did serve in that campaign. Why do you ask?'

'No special reason. Just interested. It was so long ago. At that time I had not even been born. What regiment were you in?'

Grant was surprised by this interrogation. He was also trying to understand what Gerda was driving at. He could not believe that she was asking the questions simply out of idle curiosity. There had to be some purpose. But what?

Reedham hesitated before answering. Then he said:

'I was in the Royal Artillery.'

'And were you ever in North Germany? In the late winter of nineteen forty-five perhaps?'

Reedham shook his head. 'No, I never got to that part of the front.'

'No? Well, it is of no importance.'

He was still looking at her closely, still apparently trying to probe behind the mask of her face and read the contents of her mind. And he was uneasy; there could be no doubt about that. She had stirred something in him, touched a nerve, conjured up some long hidden fear perhaps, a phantom from the past. His glance seemed to be saying: 'Who are you? What do you want of me?' But he was not going to have the answer. Not yet.

And then she got to her feet. 'We have taken up too much of your valuable time, Mr Reedham. We must leave now.'

He made no attempt to detain them; no doubt he was glad they were going. He himself conducted them to the door, perhaps to make certain that they really did leave the premises.

On the doorstep Grant turned to him and said: 'Incidentally, you may be interested to know that *Bavarian Sunset* was recently sold by auction. It'll probably find its way to America, if it is not already there.'

It seemed to come as news to Reedham. 'How did you know it was mine?' he asked. 'I don't imagine it was entered under my name.'

'Oh, didn't I tell you? I know the man who stole it from you. I managed to persuade him to tell me where he got it. Funny the way things turn out sometimes, isn't it?'

The expression on Reedham's face seemed to indicate that he found nothing whatever funny about it. He was certainly not laughing; in fact he looked distinctly sour.

'Well, goodbye,' Grant said. 'Perhaps we shall be meeting again sometime.'

Reedham did not say he hoped so. He said absolutely nothing. But he could have been thinking a great deal. And not enjoying the exercise.

* * *

In the car Cynara could hardly wait to ask: 'Now what was that all about?'

Gerda replied innocently: 'What was all what about?'

'You know, those questions you were asking Reedham about his war service and what not. Why the interest in where he was in the winter of nineteen forty-five?'

'Curiosity; that's all.'

'Ah, come off it, Gerda. There was more to it than that.'

'You think so?'

'I'm sure so.'

'Well, perhaps you're right. But he was lying, of course.'

'Now how can you possibly know that?'

'I can't for certain. But I feel sure he was.'

'And I think you're right,' Grant said. 'I'd say he was lying all along the line. What's more, I doubt very much whether he was ever in the Royal Artillery.'

'What makes you think that?' Gerda asked.

'Well, in the first place he was wearing what looked very much like a regimental tie; a sort of rifle motif; and that certainly isn't the Artillery design. That's not conclusive, of course; but did you notice the framed photograph over the mantelpiece? Rows of men in khaki battledress.'

Cynara said she had seen it but had not taken much notice. Gerda had also spotted it.

'But what about it?'

'I don't suppose either of you read the inscription on the bottom.'

Apparently neither of them had.

'I was nearer to it,' Grant said, 'and I did read it. It ran like this: "Officers and men of B Company, Second Battalion, Wessex Rifles, 1944". One of the lieutenants looked remarkably like a much younger version of Mr Clifford Reedham.'

Cynara looked thoughtful. 'So why would he say he was in the Royal Artillery if in fact he was in the Wessex Rifles?'

'Good question. And the only possible answer that springs to mind – to my mind anyway – is that for some reason or other he didn't want us to know just where in Europe he was serving at the end of the War. The Artillery were everywhere. It's on their cap badge, isn't it? Ubique. But a regiment like the Wessex Rifles would be easier to pin down.'

'And do you know where they were at that time?' Gerda asked. 'The Second Battalion in particular.'

'No, I don't. But I could probably find out.'

'I wish you would do that,' she said.

* * *

In Marley Hall Reedham was having a talk with his man, Cragg; and it was not a happy discussion.

'They're on to me,' Reedham said. 'No doubt about it.'

'How do you know?' Cragg asked. 'What did they say?'

'It was the German woman; she was the one; the other two were just helping her. I don't know how much she'd told them; maybe all they knew was that she was looking for the person who brought that painting out of Germany. Of course she told some story about doing research for a book about the artist, but that was just eyewash.'

'But how could she be connected? She wouldn't have been born till years after. And the name ain't right, is it? Hoffmann, I mean. That woman said her name was Neuberg, as I recall.'

'I know she did.' Reedham spoke petulantly. 'But that means nothing. And why would this one have wanted to know whether I was in North Germany in the winter of nineteen forty-five if she didn't know what happened at that time?'

'She asked that, did she?'

'Yes.'

'You didn't tell her, did you?'

'Talk sense. I'm not as stupid as that. I said I was in the Royal Artillery and never in those parts. I'm not sure she believed it, though.'

Cragg gave a shrug. 'What's it matter anyway? It was all a long time ago. What can anybody do about it now?'

'I don't know. But there was a boy, remember. He'll be a man now. In his fifties. And it was his mother, don't forget.'

'So what of it? If he was going to do anything about it he'd have done it long before this.'

'And perhaps he would have done if he could have found me. Perhaps he's been looking. Perhaps it was that picture coming up for sale that gave him the clue he needed.'

'But it ain't him, is it? It's a girl.'

'There could be a connection.'

'You worry too much,' Cragg said. 'And even if there is a connection, and even if somebody was to come looking for trouble with us, we can handle it.'

'We're not as young as we were.'

'Hell, don't I know! But we're not too old; not yet by a long chalk. Anyone wants trouble with us, we give 'em trouble. Right?'

Reedham did not echo Cragg's word. He was not so sure. He was younger than Cragg, but too old at that to welcome the kind of business that his man was referring to. There had been plenty of that in the past, but all he wanted now for the rest of his days was a quiet life. And now something out of the distant past had been resurrected to plague him, to take away his peace of mind and put the fear of long-deferred retribution into his heart.

'That damned painting!' In a fit of petulance he punched the arm of the chair he was sitting in with his clenched fist. 'That bloody painting!'

Cragg stood watching him with a contemptuous twist to his mouth; despising him now as he had despised him all those years ago when Reedham had been a young lieutenant, not yet dry behind the ears, and he had been a sergeant, hard-bitten and experienced.

'You'd have done better to have pinched the flippin' silver like what I did,' he said.

SIX

Opposition

That damned painting! Why had he taken it? It had been an act carried out on the spur of the moment. The thing had caught his eye and he had felt a sudden urge to possess it. So he had carried it away, never dreaming of any trouble it might bring for him half a century later. Who could have foreseen such a consequence? Who ever looked forward that length of time? No one. There had been an expression uttered many a time by Sergeant Cragg: 'To the victor the spoils.' But who in the end was the victor and who the vanquished?

Now the memories came crowding back; memories of what he had done in that room where he had gone with the woman. What fit of madness had possessed him then? It was so out of character, the brutality. He would never have suspected himself of being capable of such a deed. But was not that capability latent in every man? A wild beast lying dormant within him and waiting only for the opportunity to break loose.

And the opportunity had been there, the invitation.

Besides which, there had been the abnormality of the time: in war the ordinary civilised standards went by the board. Killing, looting, rapine; they were all part of the

77

scene, becoming commonplace by repetition. He had done no more than thousands of others had done. The woman had been one of the enemy; a thing, an object, scarcely to be regarded as a human being. So why should he have felt any remorse? Why should he have been haunted by recollection of the deed?

Yet he had been. It was a weakness in him.

And of course the act had delivered him into the hands of Sergeant Cragg, because, though Cragg had not been an eye-witness, had not been in the room, he had heard the woman scream and had seen the marks of her fingernails on his face, the blood. So he had not needed to be told what had happened in there, and he had seen the theft of the picture and could have ruined him with a word.

Not that Cragg had any reason to utter the word; his own hands were none too clean if it came to the point. Nevertheless, the feeling that a man like Cragg should have this hold on him was irksome, to say the least.

* * *

The War came to its bloody conclusion, leaving the aftermath of shattered towns and cities, the ravaged countryside, the dead; and the maimed, the bitterness and the hatred. Reedham came out of the army as soon as he was allowed to do so. He had never had any desire for a military career and his commission had been only a temporary one. He was glad to be back in civvy street and hoped that he would never again be obliged to put on a uniform.

Unfortunately, in post-war Britain there seemed to be no niche into which he could successfully insert himself. He was qualified for nothing. He got himself accommodation in an unfashionable part of London and drifted from one ill-paid job to another, assisted in the leaner periods by a grudging allowance from his father. He had taken the Arnold Sempler painting to Marley Hall, where it had been hung alongside a number of mediocre works of little value which had been in the family for years.

His father had looked at it with the eye of an unashamed philistine; being a man who was more of a judge of horseflesh than of art.

'What's this?'

'Something I picked up in Germany. Something to hang on the wall with the others.'

The old man had sniffed. 'Enough of that rubbish already.' But he had accepted the addition and *Bavarian Sunset* had remained in its new home, gathering dust with the rest of them.

* * *

Clifford Reedham had never been on the best of terms with his father, an irascible man addicted to fox-hunting and the whisky bottle. Clifford, an only child, adored by his mother and despised by his father as a namby-pamby, had been educated at a minor public school where he had achieved little, either academically or athletically, and had at an early age found himself, rather to his own surprise, with a commission in the army. It was his private opinion that the best that could be said for being a member of an officers' mess was that it was marginally less horrible than life in the ranks, which he had had to endure at the start of his brief and totally undistinguished military career.

By the time he had crossed the Channel and

advanced into Europe the enemy had already been to all intents and purposes defeated. He had seen little action and had been at times scared out of his wits, but had sustained no more serious injury than some scratches on the cheek inflicted by a woman's fingernails.

He had remained for some time in Germany with the army of occupation, and Sergeant Cragg had been close to him as his evil genius. Together they had operated in the black market, channelling military stores into the hands of illicit dealers and sailing pretty close to the wind. There had been a kind of ring, a crooked quartermaster at the centre, and they had made a packet.

How long it would have gone on before detection was followed by an inevitable court-martial was impossible to tell; but for Reedham at least it was never to be put to the test; the date of his discharge was suddenly brought forward and, leaving Cragg to serve the remainder of his engagement as a regular soldier, he departed to the land of his birth.

He had enough money in hand to lead for a time the life of a gentleman of leisure. A grateful government had set up Resettlement Advice Offices to assist discharged war heroes returning to civilian life, but this particular hero steered well clear of these and went his own sweet way. Which meant that the money soon trickled out of his pockets into those of pimps and prostitutes and various other smart operators who were adept at the art of separating a fool from his fortune. Without Cragg to help and guide him he was ill-equipped to deal with such people, and within a few weeks he was forced to make a strategic retreat from the Metropolis and take up his quarters at Marley Hall.

There, however, he immediately came into conflict

with his father, who saw no reason why he should support an idle son, war hero or not. He spoke with typical bluntness.

'Why don't you get up off your arse and work for a living?'

Such attacks as this, constantly repeated, convinced Clifford that Marley Hall was no refuge and that he would have to move out again. His mother had some money of her own, and it did not take much persuasion on his part to get her to provide him with enough of the commodity to establish himself once again in London, the magnet that would always draw him back.

This was the start of that period when he moved from one unskilled job to another and in the lean times extracted those occasional advances from his father, which were not so much allowances from a generous parent as bribes to keep him away from Marley Hall and out of that parent's thinning hair. With the bonus of a remittance now and then from his mother, unknown to her husband, he was able to keep his head above water, and he had been living in this manner for quite a few years when Arthur Cragg once again crossed his path.

* * *

It seemed like an accidental meeting, the chances of which in a conurbation the size of London must have been one in millions. He had left his cheap little flat and was strolling rather aimlessly in the direction of the City when someone came up behind him and tapped him on the shoulder. He turned and saw the man, and it took him a moment or two to realise that it was Cragg, because this was a civilian and he had never seen him dressed in anything but his army uniform.

Then the man said: 'Mr Reedham as ever was! Thought it was you. Long time, no see. How's the world treating you?'

So then he knew it was Cragg, and he was not at all sure it was a pleasure to see him, because he had a premonition that this might be a fateful meeting and that something had come back into his life which he had thought to be rid of for ever with the shedding of his khaki. A shiver ran down his spine, as if a phantom from the past had suddenly appeared before him.

'Well, well, well!' Cragg said. 'Fancy meeting you of all people! What are you doing in these parts?'

'I live near here,' Reedham said.

Cragg expressed surprise. 'You do? Wouldn't have thought this was quite your style. Somewhere more classy I'd have expected for Mr Clifford Reedham.'

Reedham detected a note of mockery and he spoke curtly. 'I have to take what comes.'

He was still amazed at the coincidence of meeting Cragg like this; it was not until later that he was to learn that it had been far from blind chance and that Cragg had in fact been waiting for him, had seen him leave his quarters and had followed him for some way before making his presence known. It had not been difficult for Cragg to discover Reedham's address: all that had been necessary had been to put through a telephone call to Marley Hall, which he knew was where the parents lived, having made a note of it years ago and kept it for possible future reference. He had spoken to Mrs Reedham, told her he was an old army friend of her son's and wished to contact him for a chat over matters of mutual interest. Mrs Reedham had been only too pleased to supply the information.

'I am sure Clifford will be delighted to renew the

acquaintance of a former comrade-in-arms.'

It had been a misjudgement, but she was not to know that.

Cragg said: 'How about you and me finding some place to have a bit of a heart-to-heart?'

Reedham demurred. 'I don't know that I have the time.'

'Sure you have. You don't kid me. Come along.'

* * *

They talked in a public-house.

Reedham said: 'Are you out of the army?'

'Yes, I'm out,' Cragg said.

'I didn't think your time would have been up yet.'

Cragg grinned, showing his big and slightly yellow teeth. 'They let me go early.'

'Are you telling me you bought yourself out?'

'Nah. It didn't cost me nothing.'

He did not mention that it had not been an honourable discharge, that in fact he had been kicked out after serving a sentence in the glasshouse, a military detention centre, where he had been sent after a court-martial. He revealed this fact only after they had had a few drinks and had talked of other things. Reedham was not altogether surprised.

'So they caught you in the end?'

'Yes, the bastards caught me. Somebody squealed.'

It occurred to Reedham that he himself had been lucky to get away before the axe fell. If he had still been there with Cragg at that time he could have got it in the neck too. But here was Cragg out and about again and suggesting that the two of them should go into partnership as before, taking up where they had left off, only in a new line of business. It scared him just to think about it, but Cragg was all for it and he knew that in the end that was the way it was going to be; he was not strong-willed enough to refuse.

*   *   *

They went into the secondhand car business; it took no vast amount of capital to start and there were opportunities to make a quick profit. After a time they acquired some old sheds and an abandoned builder's yard, and the enterprise grew. But it was not all above-board: more and more of the cars they sold were stolen goods. They went into the sheds and came out a different colour and with a new identity. There was real money in that game.

But there was competition, rival gangs in the same line of business; and there were big gang bosses who marked out their territory and tolerated no interlopers. Cragg and Reedham found themselves being warned off, and as an example to others some of their suppliers, the car thieves, were beaten up. It became increasingly difficult to obtain the goods they needed and profits slumped.

'I think we should call it a day,' Reedham said. He was unhappy with the situation. He dreaded violence.

But Cragg was made of tougher material and he was stubborn. 'Like hell we should! This is our pitch and here we stay.'

'They're turning nasty.'

'Maybe they are. And so maybe we'll turn nasty too.'

That was typical, Reedham thought; Cragg had never been one to let himself be pushed around. But he was not the only member of the firm who was likely to be pushed.

* * *

One evening Reedham was alone in the office, which was a rather cramped room at the end of one of the sheds and had a grimy window looking out on to the yard, when he had visitors. There was no one else anywhere around at this time, and they walked straight over to the office and came in without knocking, closing the door behind them. There were two of them, and one look was enough to tell Reedham that they had not come to buy a secondhand car. They were hard-looking characters in dark suits and black trilby hats. One of them had a lot of scar tissue above his eyes and could have been a boxer; the other one had a nose like the beak of an eagle and small eyes set so close together you could hardly have put the end of a finger between them.

Reedham spoke nervously: 'What can I do for you gentlemen?'

They were not gentlemen, of course; you could see that a mile off. They were thugs, bully-boys, nasties of the worst kind. And he was alone in there with them.

'It ain't what you can do for us but what we can do for you,' the hook-nosed one said.

The scar-faced one just laughed in an unpleasant kind of way but said nothing.

There was a telephone on the desk at Reedham's side, and he had a wild idea of calling the police, though in the ordinary way he would not have welcomed a policeman anywhere near the place. He had in fact, made a tentative movement of his hand towards the instrument when the hook-nosed man slammed down on his wrist with a short cosh which he had produced from an inner pocket.

It made Reedham cry out with pain; he was afraid his wrist had been broken. The man grinned at him savagely.

'That's just for starters.'

'What do you want?' Reedham's voice shook. 'What have I done to you?'

'Just being here, that's what you've done. You been warned to get out, but you ain't gone. Now you gotta be learnt a lesson.'

They started on him then. The hook-nosed man struck him on the side of the head with the cosh, and he saw a blinding display of stars and fell to the floor. The other man kicked him when he was down. He screamed; the pain was agonising. He felt the cosh again and the kicking went on. He tried to roll himself up into a ball to protect the most vulnerable parts of his body, but it did not help much. He wondered whether this was to be the end for him, whether they really meant to kill him. Whatever they intended the final result to be, they were certainly giving him a lot of punishment along the way; and for the present they were keeping him conscious so that he could feel it.

There was no telling how long this would have gone on if the men had not been interrupted in their work. But in the event they were. The door opened and Cragg came in.

'What goes on?' Cragg demanded. The question was unnecessary; it was easy enough to see what was going on. But he asked it just the same.

And it stopped the men. They turned and looked at Cragg.

'Who wants to know?' the hook-nosed man asked; the cosh in his right hand, smacking the palm of his other hand with it in a speculative kind of way. Intimidating.

Cragg was not intimidated. 'I do,' he said. 'I'm his partner.' He pointed to Reedham, who was still on the floor, moaning and making no attempt to get up.

'So you're his partner! Well now, how's that for a piece of luck! Now we can do you too. What say, Pug?'

The one called Pug was all in favour of that. 'He jus' come askin' for it. Couldn't bin better.'

'You think you can handle me?' Cragg inquired. He seemed to ask the question simply as a matter of interest, not raising his voice, cool as you like. 'Just the two of you?'

The hook-nosed man sneered. 'Tough guy, huh?'

'Maybe.'

'But not tough enough, I reckon. Let's take him, Pug.'

They made a move, but Cragg had made his move just a shade more quickly. He had slipped a hand inside his jacket and when it came out again there was a big black automatic pistol in it, a Colt .45. Reedham had seen the pistol before; an American soldier had probably carried it at one time, and somehow it had come into Cragg's possession. Since the threats of violence had been bandied about he had taken to carrying it in a leather holster under his jacket – as a precaution.

'Don't,' he said.

It stopped them for the moment. They stared at the gun. It was something they had not been expecting; a counter to the cosh and the boot, cold and menacing.

'I could kill you both. Easy.'

'You wouldn't dare.'

'Why not? You wouldn't be the first, not by a long chalk. There was a war, remember?' Cragg worked the slide of the Colt, bringing a round into the breach. The very sound of it held a menace of its own. He mocked the men. 'Come on. Come and take me. Maybe I'm bluffing; maybe I wouldn't dare shoot you. There's one sure way of finding out.'

They did not move.

Cragg taunted them again. 'What are you? A pair of

yeller-bellies? Weak at the knees, are you? Boys sent to do a man's job. Jackals, sewer rats, garbage, horse-shit –'

It was too much for them; they started to rush at him. Cragg shot the hook-nosed man in the right arm. He screamed, dropped the cosh and staggered back. It brought the other one to a stop. Cragg walked up to him and hit him on the side of the jaw with the heavy pistol. It was a vicious blow and it broke the bone. Reedham could hear the cracking sound of it, and despite his own pain he felt a surge of exultation. The bastards had dished out the punishment; now they were getting paid back in kind, and maybe with interest.

'Get going,' Cragg said. 'Go back to your kennels, you dogs. You make the place stink.'

They went. He gave them some parting kicks to speed them on their way and followed to see them off the premises. It was growing dark and they stumbled like drunken men. He heard a car start up and move away. It was being driven either by a man with a bleeding arm or one with a broken jaw; he did not care which. They would both be in pain and maybe they would head for the nearest hospital. It was a dead certainty they would not go to the police.

When he went back into the office he found that Reedham had managed to get himself on to a chair; but he was looking sick.

'How are you feeling?' Cragg asked.

'That's a stupid bloody question,' Reedham said, speaking peevishly. 'How do you think I'm feeling?'

'Bad. But you'll get over it.'

'I think I've got a cracked rib; maybe more than one. It hurts me when I breathe.'

'You want a quack to take a look at you?'

'You bet I do.'

'Okay, we'll see about it.'

'Well,' Reedham said, 'this settles it. Now we really had better clear out.'

'Why?'

'Oh, for God's sake! Don't you see? They won't stop at this. It'll get worse. I've had enough.'

'Well, I haven't,' Cragg said. 'I'm not going to let those buggers drive me out. Hell, no. It's just not on. No way.'

* * *

But two days later the place was fire-bombed and burned to the ground.

'Now what do you say?' Reedham demanded.

Even Cragg had to admit defeat. The opposition was just too strong for them; too determined to be rid of them.

'I think,' he said, 'we should take a holiday. In Spain.'

SEVEN

The Robbery Lark

They rented a villa on the Costa Brava. The floods of British holidaymakers had not yet hit the Spanish resorts and living was cheap. There were women to be had and they took life easy; basking in the sunshine, drinking the Spanish wine, making trips into Barcelona to watch the bullfighting and maybe the football. It was good while it lasted, and it might have gone on for ever if the money had not run out. But they were spending and nothing was coming in. The pot of gold melted away and the women left.

'We shall have to go back home,' Cragg said. 'No bloody alternative.'

They had enough cash left for that; enough to tide them over for a time while they looked round. Reedham put the bite on his parents and that helped. His mother begged him to pay a visit to Marley Hall; it was so long since he had been there.

He went, but did not stay long. His father was even more difficult to get on with than before, and they quarrelled vehemently. The senior Reedham was drinking more heavily, and in the son's opinion had become a cantankerous old bore who accused Clifford, not without some justification, of being a good-for-nothing, a ne'er-do-well, a layabout and a waster.

'You'll never amount to anything. No backbone. God knows how I ever came to be punished with a son like you.'

Clifford was stung into retaliation. 'And what are you? A bloody drunken old bastard. God knows how I came to be punished with such a parent.'

The barb struck home. His father's face went purple and he seemed in danger of apoplexy. He was all too aware of his own heavy drinking, but he could not bear to have anyone mention it to him. Mrs Reedham had tried at one time to persuade him to moderate his intake of whisky, but this had only thrown him into a rage and she had given up the struggle as hopeless. Now to hear himself described by this worthless whippersnapper of a son as a drunken old bastard was just too much.

'Get out,' he shouted. 'Get out of my house and don't come back. I never want to see you again.'

Despite his mother's tears, Clifford Reedham departed the next day without taking leave of his father or even catching sight of him. It was destined to be their final parting, with anger and recrimination on both sides.

*   *   *

'So,' Cragg said, 'you've had it with the old man. Me, I never knew mine. He left my ma before I was born. She's gone too now. She took to whoring and a nutter stuck a knife into her. She bled to death on a doorstep. Well, it's one of the hazards of the trade. Never know who or what you're going to pick up.'

They had decided not to go back to the secondhand

car business. They wanted no renewal of that earlier conflict; no more gang warfare. The flame was just not worth the candle.

'I got a different idea,' Cragg said. 'I know a couple of likely lads and I been talking to them. They're all for it.'

'All for what?'

'The robbery lark.'

Reedham was not at all sure he liked the sound of that. It could be dangerous; you could be caught and sent to jail. He said as much to Cragg, who brushed the objection aside.

'Break the law any way you like and if you're caught it's porridge for you. But why get caught? There's plenty as gets away with it, so why not us?'

'Well, I don't know –'

'Just meet the lads. Talk it over.'

He allowed himself to be persuaded. After all, he could always back out. There was no harm in talking.

* * *

They had both been in the army. Commandos. They were tough boys. Their names were Joe Barfield and Steve Lock. Cragg introduced Reedham to them in a pub. They looked at him and he could tell they were not impressed.

'So you're Cliff Reedham,' Barfield said. 'Arthur's been telling us about you.'

Reedham wondered just what Cragg had told them. Not, he hoped, about that business in Germany.

Barfield was lean and taller than average. He looked strong; there was a kind of controlled tension in him, like a spring wound up and ready to uncoil. He was quite handsome too in a rugged sort of way: pale blond hair, clean-cut features, blue eyes. Someone to charm the ladies and maybe lead them later to tears and lamentation. There was a steely coldness in those eyes.

Lock was a contrast to him: short and stocky, chubby-featured, inclined to grin a lot, as if he found most things in life just one big joke. They were both about the same age as Reedham, but he would have said there was little else in common between them and him.

In that group he felt like the odd man out. He came from a totally different background and he did not even speak like the others. He wondered why Barfield and Lock would even consider operating with someone like him, and he came to the conclusion that it could only be because Cragg had persuaded them that he was a worthy member of the team. Later he discovered that he had been picked for a particular job – driving. He was to be the wheelman, the driver of the getaway car.

'It's just up your street,' Cragg said. 'You're a pretty smart driver. You can handle a car like nobody's business.'

It was the truth. He loved fast cars, always had. And he really could handle them. Time was when he had had visions of becoming a racing driver, somebody like Nuvolari or Dick Seaman. He had been young then, and of course it had never been more than a dream. Then the War had come and that had altered everything. But yes, he could drive.

So on Cragg's recommendation the others accepted him; but only, he felt, with reservations. He doubted whether they ever trusted him completely; but they had to rely on him for a rapid departure whenever they did a job.

It frightened him. He was on edge all the time he was waiting for them to come running. But there was a feeling of exhilaration too, especially when they were moving, maybe weaving in and out of traffic, getting away fast from the scene of the crime in a stolen car. It was always stolen, always one with plenty of speed, like a Jaguar or a Mercedes or some such, which would be abandoned later when they switched to another vehicle.

The first job they carried out was on a bank in a small country town, and it was so easy it was hardly believable. Cragg, Barfield and Lock went into the bank with Balaclava helmets on their heads. Cragg had a sawn-off shotgun and the other two had handguns. There were about a dozen customers in the bank, and they were herded up to one end and ordered to lie down, faces to the floor. They did as they were told, none of them attempting anything heroic. The cashiers were co-operative too; they just stuffed money into the bags the robbers had brought as fast as they could. It was not their money and they were not going to risk dying for it.

To Reedham, waiting in the black Jaguar outside with the engine running, it seemed like an age before the others ran out of the bank with the guns and the loot. They all piled into the car and he got it away while they were still shutting the doors.

There was a main road running through the town and most of the shops and other places of business, including the bank, were strung along it. It was rather congested with traffic, and that was where he had to use his driving skill, putting on the pace but avoiding any sort of collision which could have been disastrous. And he did it well; in a very short time they were clear of the town and he kept going on the main road for about a couple of miles before turning off on to a minor one which was narrow and winding but not so busy. They had one shock when they came round a bend and found

a farm tractor with a harrow blocking the way. It looked
as if they were going to hit it, but he took the car up on
to the grass verge and scraped past by a whisker, leaving
the tractor driver gaping.

After that it was all plain sailing and Barfield
complimented him on a neat piece of work.

'Nice going, Cliff. Looks like we really got ourselves a
wheelman.'

It was the first bit of praise he had had from that
quarter and he felt a glow of pride. It was more than he
would ever have expected, a kind of acceptance of him
as a valued member of the gang.

'Don't flatter him,' Cragg said. 'It'll go to his head.'
But it was just a joke; he was pleased too. After all he
had recommended the wheelman.

The other car was where they had left it, at the side of
a quiet country lane on the edge of a wood. They made
the transfer quickly, and no other traffic came along
while they were doing it. A minute or two later they
were on their way back to London, not speeding, not
doing anything to draw attention to themselves. It had
been a really smooth job from start to finish.

The take was not big, just a few thousands. But the
ease with which it had been obtained made the exercise
worth while. Maybe if they had been content to continue
making small-scale raids – sub-post offices, branch
banks, filling-stations and the like – working out in the
sticks, as Cragg put it, and steering clear of big towns
and city centres, all might have gone well. But Barfield
and Lock got tired of that; they wanted to go for bigger
game.

'This is just chicken-feed,' Barfield said. 'Why don't
we try for something more profitable?'

'Because,' Cragg said, 'the bigger the job, the bigger

the risk. So this way we don't make the top money; okay, that's so; I grant you that. But we don't get nabbed neither.'

Lock sneered: 'So you're afraid of the risk?'

Reedham could see that this got under Cragg's skin. It was an accusation of faint-heartedness that was bound to rouse his temper. But he kept himself under control and answered calmly: 'It's not a question of being afraid; it's a choice between using your loaf and being plain bloody stupid.'

'What's so stupid about going for the bigger prizes? That way we can maybe earn ourselves a nice little holiday in the sun.'

'Or in one of Her Majesty's hotels. On the Isle of Wight maybe.'

They argued about it, and Lock was backing Barfield all the way. Reedham was saying nothing, and they were not asking for his opinion; it was as if he did not count. And finally Cragg gave way, perhaps because he was still smarting from the suggestion that he was yellow and felt the need to prove that he was not. Which was probably as bad a reason as any for changing his stance.

* * *

The choice was a jeweller's shop in North London. It was in a narrow lane and there was nothing very impressive about it. But Barfield had taken a look at it and had reported that there was plenty of valuable stuff on display inside.

'It'll be a cinch,' he said. 'Quick in, quick out and away. Nothing to it.'

'Maybe,' Cragg said. He was still feeling sour about

the change of work pattern, though he was ready to play his part.

It was about five o'clock in the afternoon and was getting dark when Reedham brought the stolen Citroën to a halt just a few yards away from the entrance to the shop. The other three got out. They were wearing hats and dark glasses, but no Balaclava helmets, which would have made them conspicuous. Cragg had the sawn-off shotgun under the car coat he was wearing and his companions had the handguns in their pockets. Reedham had parked the car by the kerb so that he had a clear view of the shop door, and he saw the men go inside. Then he waited, heart beating fast, sweating a little, dead scared, because he was never able to get used to it, never able to take the thing coolly as just an ordinary job of work.

The seconds ticked by and there was no sound from inside the shop, which was a good sign. He just hoped that everything was going smoothly in there; the staff co-operating, not setting off any alarms, filling the bags with jewellery; customers heeding the threat of the guns and not interfering.

As always, the operation seemed to take one hell of a long time. People went past on the pavement. No one went into the shop. A delivery van came up the lane and parked just ahead of the Citroën. Reedham viewed it with misgiving. He would have to pull out sharply to get past it, and if anything were approaching from the opposite direction at the time it would block the way. And still the others had not come out of the shop. What was holding them? Surely they should have finished the job by now.

Then he saw the policeman appear in the driving mirror. The policeman was advancing along the pavement at a steady pace, not hurrying. He paused when he drew level with the rear of the Citroën and halted. He seemed to be reading the registration number. The number plate was a false one; they had changed the plates after stealing the car; it was their regular practice. But for some reason or other the policeman appeared to be suspicious; he came up to the door and peered in at Reedham, making a signal to him to lower the window. Reedham did so.

'Would you mind telling me, sir, why you've got the engine running?'

'I'm waiting for someone,' Reedham said; croakingly, his throat feeling dry.

'You could wait with the engine stopped.'

'It's hard to start. The battery's low.'

'Hm!' the policeman said. He seemed to be taking this explanation with a certain amount of doubt. 'This is your car, is it, sir?'

'Yes, it's mine.'

'Would you mind showing me your driving licence, sir?'

Reedham was in a panic. If he produced the licence the man would know his name, and even if he got away after the robbery he would be a hunted man. But the policeman was waiting and he had to do something. He put a hand inside his jacket, fumbling in the pocket. He could feel his wallet with the licence inside it, but he did not pull it out.

'I'm sorry, officer. I don't seem to have it on me.'

'You don't seem to have it on you. I see.'

There was no doubt about the policeman's suspicion now. He had a pocket radio and he began to speak into it. Reedham saw that everything was going wrong; the man was going to report to the station, and that could be disastrous. Reedham tried to think of a way out of the predicament, but nothing came into his head. What could he do? What on earth could he do?

And then suddenly the problem was not his any longer, because the door of the shop opened and out came the robbers; Cragg carrying the sawn-off shotgun and Lock with one bag of jewellery and Barfield with another. The policeman turned and saw them. Cragg was nearest to him, and he did not hesitate but grappled with him before Cragg could even think of using the gun.

The constable was a big strong man, and he was a good match for Cragg. In the struggle the two of them fell to the ground, the constable on top, holding Cragg and trying to prevent him from using the firearm.

Neither Barfield nor Lock went to Cragg's aid. They piled into the back of the car and slammed the door.

'Let's go,' Barfield yelled. 'Let's go.'

Reedham hesitated. 'What about Arthur?'

'Damn him. He'll have to take his chance. Step on it.'

Cragg and the constable appeared to be still grappling on the pavement, locked in a far from loving embrace. Cragg could obviously have used some help, but no one was obliging. Reedham thought about it, but that was as far as he got. He felt something hard and cold pressing into the back of his neck, and he knew that it was a gun.

'Get moving,' Barfield snarled, 'or I'll blow your stinking head off.'

Reason might have told Reedham that he would do no such thing, since it would have been a perfect way of making certain that the car did not move. But Reedham was in no state to reason coolly, and he was eager to get away too. So he hesitated no longer, but got the car going. And just as he did so he heard the gun go off and knew that Cragg must have shot the policeman.

EIGHT

Surprise, Surprise!

He split up with Barfield and Lock after the raid on the jeweller's. The three of them had got away all right, but Cragg had been taken. As it turned out, he had not shot the policeman; the gun had gone off without harming anyone. And then a member of the public had lent a hand and enabled the constable to put the cuffs on Cragg.

So there he was in custody and maybe helping himself by implicating the rest of the gang. He would have had every excuse for doing so, seeing that they had made their getaway and left him to fend for himself. Reedham lived for days in fear of imminent arrest, but nothing happened, so gradually he began to breathe more freely and came to the conclusion that Cragg, for reasons best known to himself, had refused to put the finger on his accomplices. It was amazing, and Reedham did not believe it had anything whatever to do with honour among thieves; such a concept would never have found a place in Cragg's book. So he must have had some other motive, though what it might be was a mystery.

But Reedham had had a fright and had lost the taste

for a life of crime. He did not even take his share of the jewellery. Where would he have sold it? And would it not have been a risk even to handle it?

He was once more in Spain when Cragg's trial came up. He had enough money to last for a while if he lived in a modest style. And in Spain he felt safe. He read about Cragg's trial in an English newspaper. The charge was armed robbery, and the only possible verdict was one of guilty. The sentence was heavy and Reedham felt the shock, knowing as he did that he might have got the same if luck had not been with him and if Cragg had not kept his mouth shut.

He stayed in Spain for quite a while, but even the most stringent economy could not ensure that his limited supply of money would last for ever. His purse was no widow's cruse, and after a time he found himself once again nearing the end of his resources. In this predicament he could think of only one course of action: he would have to write to his parents and beg for a handout. He had not been in touch with them at all since his departure for Spain, and it would be news to them that he had gone abroad. He had a feeling that his father might be willing to pay a price to keep him there, and he was sure that his mother would chip in with a generous amount.

Having posted his begging letters he waited in impatient expectation of a speedy reaction. Several days passed, however, and nothing came. Surely, he thought, they could not intend simply to ignore him. His father, of course, might well be ill-natured enough to let him stew for a while in his own juice as a way of punishing him, but he did not believe that his mother would hesitate to respond to his plea.

But still nothing came, and he was beginning to

despair when an official-looking envelope with his name and address typewritten on it arrived from England. Opening it, he discovered that inside was a letter from a firm of solicitors informing him that his parents had both been killed in a motoring accident and that he was the heir to the estate. The solicitors regretted that they had been unable to get in touch with him earlier, but until his letter had been forwarded to them they had been ignorant of his present whereabouts, and so on.

He prepared at once to leave Spain and return to England. The solicitors had given no details of the motoring accident in which his parents had lost their lives, but he was to learn later that no other vehicle had been involved. His father had been driving his car along one of the narrow lanes not far from Marley Hall, had taken a sharp bend at far too great a speed and had lost control. The car had broken through a wooden fence and had plunged into a disused gravel-pit. Whether the occupants had been killed by the impact or had died in the subsequent fire was not known.

Reedham did not need to be told why the accident had occurred. He could guess that his father had been drinking heavily, and the result had been fatal. He had no regrets concerning the death of the old man; in his opinion it was good riddance to bad rubbish; but it was a pity that his mother had been involved. Still, there was nothing to be done about that now; and at least his pecuniary problems had been solved for the present; for which dispensation of fate he was extremely grateful.

The sum of money that would be coming to him was not inconsiderable, and there was besides the hall and the estate. He was a little surprised that his father should have named him as sole legatee; he would rather have expected to have been cut out of the will altogether, knowing with what detestation the elder Reedham regarded him, especially towards the end of his life. But perhaps the will had been made out a long time ago when relations between the two of them had not deteriorated to such an extent as was to be the case later. And perhaps his father had intended changing it but had been too negligent to do so. One way or another, the fact remained that he was now quite well off and there was no need for him to go looking for a job or joining up with a gang of criminals – even if that had been feasible now that Cragg was safely stowed away in prison.

The idea of paying Cragg a visit flitted momentarily into his head, but was immediately dismissed. Such a move would undoubtedly have put the spotlight on him, and nothing could have been better calculated to draw attention in his direction. No; it would be advisable to give Cragg a wide berth and make no contact of any kind with the convicted man. It was pretty certain that Barfield and Lock would not be putting themselves out to give him the pleasure of their company during visiting hours.

And besides, why should he wish to see Cragg anyway? He had never liked the man, even though they had been close associates in the past. Indeed, he hoped that he might never see Arthur Cragg again as long as he lived. He doubted whether that hope would be fulfilled, but at least the fellow was out of the way for some years to come and he was free to enjoy his legacy with no danger of interference from that quarter.

And this he proceeded to do.

* * *

He left Marley Hall in the care of an elderly couple named Grimble, and having rented a flat in London proceeded to live it up as a gentleman of leisure. He lavished money on women; he gambled; he went to race meetings and betted heavily and disastrously on the wrong horses; he bought a red Ferrari and drove it here, there and everywhere with utter abandon and little regard for the speed limit. It was as though he were hell-bent on getting rid of his inheritance in the shortest possible time; and in this at least he was succeeding only too well.

It could not last. He ran into debt. In a vain attempt to recoup his losses he gambled even more heavily and lost money that he did not possess. To pay off the gambling debts he resorted to loan sharks and borrowed at a crippling rate of interest. When he could not pay the loan sharks they put the frighteners on him.

Two bruisers paid a call on him at his flat, and it was like a re-run of that time when two thugs had walked in on him at the used car establishment years ago. The difference was that on this occasion there was no Arthur Cragg to step in and rescue him, because Cragg was somewhere far away in a narrow cell waiting for the long slow hours to pass until he should once again be a free man. Never had Reedham so longed to see Cragg's ugly face as then, when there was no possibility of doing so.

As soon as he opened the door of the flat he knew that it was a mistake; he should never have let them in. But by then it was too late; they had simply walked in, brushing him aside and closing the door behind them.

'You bin a naughty boy,' one of them said. 'You borrowed money and you ain't paid it back. You ain't even paid the innerest. That's bad, that is.'

Reedham knew then who they had come from, and he felt sick. He answered weakly: 'I'm going to. I just need time.'

'You've 'ad all the time you're going to get,' the man said. 'Our people don't like waiting for ever; it ain't the way they do business. Unnerstand?'

Reedham understood only too well. He said: 'Look, I'll pay tomorrow. I've got some money coming in. Call again then.' He would have said anything to put them off. Tomorrow he could be gone.

They just laughed in a nasty sort of way. It seemed to be one huge joke to them.

'Now try pulling the other one,' the man said. 'It's got bells on it.'

His partner was saying not a word. Maybe he was dumb.

Reedham tried pleading. 'Please! You don't have to do this.' He did not specify what "this" was. They all knew.

'Oh, but we do,' the man said. 'Gotta earn our pay.'

They started on him then. When he tried to cry out for help they stuffed a gag in his mouth which nearly choked him. Soon they were giving him a lot of pain and he knew he was going to have some pretty bad bruises afterwards; but they were not touching his head, and it seemed as if they were being careful not to inflict any lasting damage. When they had finished the speaking man said:

'This is just a friendly warning. Next time it could be a lot worse. If I was you, Mr Reedham, I'd really see about getting that there money what you owe. You don't wanter end up a cripple, do you? Or maybe dead.'

After that they left him to think things over.

*   *   *

The next day he went round to see the loan sharks and offer an arrangement. It was his money they were after, not his blood, and they agreed to his proposal. As a result he sold off part of the Marley Hall estate and paid up.

But it was the end of the high life. He gave up the London flat and retired to Marley Hall in the Hertfordshire countryside to be looked after by the Grimbles. He was not destitute and would never be, because his mother, with admirable foresight, based no doubt on a shrewd assessment of his character, had left her own estate so cleverly tied up legally that he could draw from it only a steady, though limited, income and could not touch the capital. On this income he was able to live at Marley Hall in a modest style but in reasonable comfort.

It was a dull life; that could not be denied; but he felt that he had had enough excitement and wanted no more of it. That sort of thing was all very well when you were young, but he was now approaching fifty and maybe it was time to change his ways. Looking back he had to admit that he had hardly made a success of his career. He had had chances but had let them slip through his fingers. With the advantages that he had had another man might have achieved much, built up a commercial empire, made millions; but what had he done? Thrown everything away in the pursuit of brief pleasure. So here he was, washed up, high and dry, with nothing to look forward to but a wretched old age.

He thought of marriage. To someone with money, naturally. A rich wife would mend his fortune. But where could he find a woman with the required assets who would be willing to hitch her wagon to a man who had never had any great physical attraction at the best of times and was now, with his receding hair, pouches under the eyes and sagging chin, beginning to look decidedly seedy? It was not as if he had a wide circle of acquaintances; most of his life had been spent away from Marley Hall and he was practically unknown in the county. He did not attend social gatherings or ride to hounds as his father had done, and he had scarcely any contact with those of his own class. The fact was that he had become something of a recluse and no longer had any desire to meet people.

*   *   *

He had been leading this kind of existence for some years when Cragg turned up. It was Grimble who answered the door, and Cragg just said: 'I'm Arthur Cragg. I want to see Mr Reedham.'

The old manservant said he would go and see whether Mr Reedham was available, but Cragg did not wait for that; he followed Grimble to the room where Reedham was sitting and before he could be properly announced he was there, brushing past the servant and planting himself foursquare in front of the master.

It was a shock for the latter. Reedham had always feared that one day Cragg would walk in on him, but he had cherished a faint shred of hope that this would not happen. Perhaps the man had died in prison; if not, perhaps he would feel no urge to meet his erstwhile partner; perhaps he would commit some petty crime that would send him straight back inside. But in the event things were not to turn out in any way that he might have hoped, and here the man was, looking older of course, his hair turned quite white, but just as big, just as strong and just as menacing as ever.

'You!'

'Yes, me. Surprise, surprise!'

Reedham made a signal to Grimble and the old man retired, though not without glancing askance at the visitor.

'So,' Cragg said, 'this is where you got yourself holed up. Not bad. Could be a whole lot worse. And it's all yours now, I reckon. Seein' as how the old folks is dead.'

'How did you know that?'

'Oh, I bin making inquiries in the village. They tell me you're living here with just a couple of old servants. They say you threw a fortune away on riotous living; fast women and slow gee-gees and all that. So then you had to sell a good part of the estate to pay off your debts. Is that right?'

It came as a revelation to Reedham that so much should have been known about his affairs in Madden-hall Superior, but he supposed things like that were bound to leak out somehow or other. And what people did not know for a certainty they filled in with shrewd guesswork.

He did not trouble to deny the bare facts. 'And you? How long have you been out?'

'Not long.' Cragg sat down in an armchair facing Reedham. 'Might've bin sooner if I'd behaved meself inside. But I got caught up in some trouble and they added a bit on.'

He did not say what the trouble was. It could have been a prison riot or maybe an assault on a warder; some kind of violence almost certainly. Reedham did not need to ask how Cragg had found him; the man would have remembered the address of Marley Hall and would have reasoned that it was the most likely place to start looking for his ex-partner.

He looked at Cragg warily, a trifle apprehensively. 'What do you propose to do now?' He could not forget that Cragg had been left in the lurch after that jewel robbery. And he was damned sure Cragg had not forgotten about it either.

'I'll tell you one thing I don't propose to do,' Cragg said, 'and that's go back inside. I've had a gutful of stir and I don't aim to have no more of it.'

'You'll be looking for a job then?'

'I might be. And I mightn't have to look all that far neither. See what I mean?'

Reedham was not at all sure he cared for the sound of that. He had the distinct impression that Cragg was proposing to move into Marley Hall; and that would not be to his liking at all.

Then suddenly, without warning, Cragg jumped up from his chair, rushed at Reedham and gripped him by the throat.

'You bastard! You drove off and left me to the coppers. You left me to rot in stir while you and them other two bleeders took off with the loot. All these years I've had to think about it, and it ain't bin nice, not at all, it ain't. So give me one good reason why I shouldn't croak you, you bugger. Come on, just one reason.'

Reedham, with Cragg's large hands, which seemed to have lost none of their strength over the years, gripping his throat and closing up his windpipe, could not utter a word; he could scarcely breathe. Cragg's weight was on him, holding him down in the chair, and all he could do was flutter his own hands in a kind of mute appeal for mercy.

Cragg seemed to realise that it was no use demanding

an answer from a man he was rapidly choking to death, and he relaxed his grasp to some extent.

'Well, let's have it.'

Reedham croaked: 'It wasn't my fault. They made me.'

'Wotcher mean, made you?'

'They yelled at me to drive away, and Joe Barfield stuck a gun in the back of my neck and threatened to blow my head off if I didn't step on it.'

Cragg loosened his grip a bit more and spoke musingly: 'Yes, I guessed it was something like that. And you were too lily-livered to refuse.'

'I'd have been a dead man if I had.'

'Maybe. And maybe you'll be a dead man anyway. I bin waiting a long time. And thinking.'

Reedham could guess how it had been. All that time in prison Cragg must have been brooding over what had happened one afternoon in North London when he had been betrayed by his comrades. Brooding and planning revenge. That was why he had not squealed to the law, had not grassed on the other three. Because he had to avenge himself in his own way, with his own hands. Because he was Arthur Cragg and that was the way he did things.

Cragg lifted himself off Reedham and returned to his own chair. He was calm again, the sudden fit of rage having quickly spent itself. Reedham massaged his throat, watching him.

'So,' Cragg said, 'what am I going to do, you ask. Well, for a start I have some business in London to attend to. I shall need some money for expenses. I reckon you could let me have a bit.'

'Yes, I could manage that, if you're not wanting too much. I'm not a rich man, you know. My income is strictly limited.'

'Too bad. Because you owe me. I never did get my share of them sparklers.'

'Nor did I. I let Joe and Steve take the lot.'

Cragg stared at him in amazement. 'Why in hell did you do that?'

'I don't know. I just felt sick of the whole thing. I told them I wanted no more to do with them, and I haven't seen either of them since.'

'So you don't know where they're hanging out?'

'No.'

'Pity. I was thinking you would. Well, I shall just have to do some sniffing around, shan't I?'

Reedham looked at him uneasily. 'So you want to find them, do you?'

Cragg gave an evil grin that was more like a noiseless snarl. 'What do you think?'

Reedham tried not to think about it. It sent shivers down his spine.

*   *   *

Cragg stayed the night at Marley Hall and left early in the morning. He had no transport of his own, so Reedham drove him as far as Barnet in the old Vauxhall he now used for himself. From Barnet he could take the Underground into London.

'Well,' Cragg said as they parted, 'so long for now. I'll be seeing you.'

Reedham feared that this was only too true. Now that Cragg had turned up again he was afraid he was stuck with the man. And it did not please him in the least.

NINE

Worrying

Joe Barfield was drinking in a public-house called The Miller's Arms. He was alone and he was not feeling at all happy. Things had not been going too well with him for some time. He was on his own now, a loner, picking up a living as best he could. And it was not a fat living; the good times seemed to be past and gone for him. The fact was, he had never made much money since that jewellery job which had gone so badly wrong.

It had given him a scare, that. And not only him but Steve too. They had decided then to pack in the life of crime, because it was almost inevitable that they would eventually finish up where Cragg was if they carried on with it. You could get away with things for a time, but there was too much risk and the odds were that you would sooner or later be caught and made to pay the price.

So they had sold the jewels to a fence for a fraction of what they were worth and like Reedham had gone abroad and kept their heads down until the money ran out. After that they had returned to London and joined up with a group of mercenaries who were being taken on to fight in Africa for a cause in which they had no ideological interest whatever. It was the money that attracted them and nothing else. And the money was no great shakes at that.

It was a hell of a life.

'We'd have done better to have joined the French Foreign Legion,' Lock said. 'Damned if we wouldn't.'

He could have been right. He might have lived longer. As it was, he got a bullet in the lung and died in considerable pain in a stinking jungle swamp far away from England, home and beauty.

Barfield had lost the taste for fighting in an African war after that and had pulled out as soon as he could. But back in England he had found the going tough. The trouble was that a trained fighting man was not well qualified for jobs that demanded quite a different set of skills from those he had learned. So it became a choice between unskilled employment, often temporary and always poorly paid, and the life of crime which he had abandoned years ago.

In the event he settled for a combination of both: he who had once been a proud Commando had now sunk to the level of a casual labourer and petty thief. He was also an informer and risked the enmity of more successful criminals by snouting for a detective in the Metropolitan Police. He had to admit to himself that he could not sink much lower than that.

So it was that he did his drinking alone more often than not, and enjoyed the pleasure of female company only on those infrequent occasions when he had the money to pay for it.

Sitting now in a corner of the bar at The Miller's Arms, morosely running over in his mind the steps by which he had come to his present unhappy state and wallowing in self-pity, he failed even to notice a rugged man in dark glasses, with a crop of white hair, who was seated not far away and was unobtrusively observing him. Even if he had glanced at this individual he might well have failed to recognise in him an old acquaintance named Arthur Cragg; but Cragg recognised him and felt a certain grim satisfaction in doing so.

When Barfield rose to go Cragg watched him leave and then got up and followed him. Outside he removed the dark glasses and in the light of the street-lamps he spotted Barfield at once, slouching along the pavement some twenty yards away. Cragg fell into step behind him.

Barfield was not walking very fast, and Cragg could have overtaken him whenever he wished; but for a while he preferred merely to keep pace with him, savouring a kind of exultation in the knowledge that his moment had at last come. This went on for a couple of blocks, the quarry blissfully unaware that he was being followed and therefore feeling no uneasiness on that account.

But eventually Cragg tired of the cat-and-mouse game in which the mouse did not even know that there was a cat within striking distance, and he quickened his pace to bring him up to Barfield's left shoulder.

'Hello, Joe,' he said. 'Long time, no see.'

Barfield came to an abrupt halt. This was a voice coming out of the past; one he had not heard in years, but remembered only too well. His head jerked to the left; his eyes took in the bony features, the coarse white hair.

'Arthur!'

'Yes, Joe; Arthur Cragg as ever was. Thought you'd never see me again, maybe? Hoped you never would? Remember the way we parted all that long time ago?'

'I remember,' Barfield said.

"Course you do. Not a thing you'd be likely to forget. I remember it too. I bin remembering it all these years, I have. Waiting. Didn't have much else to do but remember how some old pals left me in the lurch. And wait.'

Barfield's voice was slightly hoarse. 'What you want with me, Arthur?' He seemed nervous.

'A talk, Joe. Just a heart-to-heart talk.'

'What about?'

'Old times maybe. Just two old buddies getting together after a long, long parting. Should be plenty of things to natter about, don't you think? Let's walk.'

He put a hand on Barfield's arm, urging him forward. Barfield made no resistance.

'How you doing these days, Joe?'

'Bloody bad, if you want the truth.'

'Dear, dear! Sorry to hear that. Thought you might've done real well for yourself with the start you got from that jewellery job. Thought you might've used it as a foundation to build your fortune on.'

Cragg was being sarcastic, but Barfield did not appreciate the sarcasm. 'Oh, very funny.'

'So you didn't make your fortune?'

'Does it look like it?'

'You're not telling me you're skint?'

'As near as makes no difference.'

Cragg made tut-tutting noises. 'Now that is a pity. 'Cause here was me thinking you'd have my share of the take all nice an' ready to hand over. But maybe you have; maybe you put it away somewhere safe and never touched it after, knowing as how it was mine by rights. Is that the way things are, Joe old pal?'

Barfield said nothing.

'Down here,' Cragg said. They had come to a

side-turning where a narrow street led off to the right. Barfield seemed reluctant to leave the better lighted and more frequented way they had been following, but Cragg was insistent and again he allowed himself to be persuaded by the other man.

It was a crooked lane, sloping downhill. There were no shops, just what looked like business premises shut up at this time of night. Few people. They came to an alleyway on the left, apparently giving access to a courtyard. Again Cragg gave the order.

'In here.'

There was no one about, the lighting poor. They came to a halt and Cragg said:

'So am I to take it that you haven't got my share?'

Barfield tried to excuse himself. 'Well, you know how it is. We always meant you to have it, straight we did, but somehow –'

'Somehow you just spent it? Sure, I know how it is, you bloody bastards.' Cragg's voice had hardened, the anger showing now. 'You made off and left me to the coppers, left me to face the music all on my ownsome. And not content with that, you took my share for yourselves. No need to bother about old Arthur, was there? He was safe behind bars. He'd be out of the way for years. But you forgot something, Joe; you forgot I'd be coming out some day and be looking for you. Because I didn't forget nothing, see? Well, you took some finding, but I guessed you might be somewhere around the old haunts, and I had the time. I kept hunting and hunting, and finally I found you, di'n't I?'

'Okay, so now you've found me.' Barfield spoke defiantly, not so nervous now. The initial shock of seeing Cragg had worn off and he knew that he was as strong as the other man and if it came to a fight he could look after himself. 'So what are you going to do about it?'

'Oh,' Cragg said, 'we'll come to that, all in good time. But first let's talk about someone else; a character named Steve Lock. You were mates, remember?'

'Sure, I remember.'

'And still are maybe?'

'No. Not any more.'

'Is that a fact? So you split up?'

'You could say that.'

'But you know where he is perhaps?'

'Yes, I know.'

'So tell me.'

'Why should I?' Barfield said. 'You do some more nosing around. Maybe you'll find him and maybe you won't.'

'No,' Cragg said, 'that won't do. I'm not going to do any more hunting. And why? Because you're going to point me to him.'

Barfield sneered. 'What makes you so sure?'

'This,' Cragg said. And suddenly there was a knife in his hand, the long pointed blade just visible to Barfield when he glanced down to see what was making that slight pressure on the lower part of his stomach. It made him shudder.

'Don't move,' Cragg said. 'Stay right where you are, or else you might get yourself sliced up real bad and never be the same man again. Now tell me where I can find Steve Lock. Is he in London?'

'No,' Barfield said; and his voice was shaking slightly. 'He ain't in London and he ain't in England.'

'Then where is he?'

'Africa.'

'Africa! What in hell's he doing there?'

'Nothing. And if you go there you won't find him, because he's in a swamp in the jungle. Nothing let of him but bones now, I guess. It's been years.'

'Is this on the up and up?'

'Sure, it is. We was fighting out there. Mercenaries. He got shot. That's all there is to it.'

Cragg believed him and felt cheated. So Lock had escaped him, robbed him of the full quota of his revenge. All those years in prison, waiting and planning how he would deal with these men, and now one of them had slipped through his fingers. It filled him with rage.

'The bastard!'

But there was one left; one right here; one who would have to pay for both. It was not enough but it would have to do. In blinding anger he thrust the knife into Joe Barfield. The man gave one thin scream and fell.

*　*　*

Reedham asked no questions when Cragg returned to Marley Hall. He thought about doing so, but then he saw the look in Cragg's eyes and thought again. That look discouraged all inquiry into what Cragg had done in London. Whether he had found Barfield and Lock, and if so what had passed between them, he appeared to be in no mood to divulge. And in a way Reedham felt it was better thus; he was not at all sure he wanted to know too much.

Cragg had been away for quite a time, and he had begun to entertain faint hopes that the man might be gone for good, never to return. But he had known in his heart that any such expectation was vain; like an Old Man of the Sea, Cragg was on his shoulders for evermore and could not be shaken off.

The question of whether or not Cragg would be staying on at Marley Hall was never discussed; there just seemed to be a tacit agreement that he would. There was ample accommodation; that was certainly no problem; and the monotony and dullness of the life appeared not to bother him. He was no longer young, and perhaps he wanted no more excitement; he had said he had no intention of ever going back to prison, so maybe he just wished to settle down and take things quietly. He had apparently completed his business in London and Reedham hoped there would be no repercussions as a result, because he himself might become involved. But no doubt Cragg had been careful.

It was not long before the Grimbles handed in their notice and left. They could not get on with Cragg, and Reedham suspected that he had purposely made himself objectionable to the old couple in order to persuade them to leave. After the departure of these last two survivors from the staff of servants that had once been employed at the hall Reedham thought of trying to engage some replacements, but Cragg, when told of the idea, was dead against it.

'Wotcher wanter do that for? I'm here, ain't I? I can see to all that needs doing. And you can pay me. It'll be the best arrangement.'

Reedham had doubts, but he could see that Cragg meant to have it his way, and that if any other servants were to be engaged he would see to it that they left again pretty smartly. He knew that he was under Cragg's thumb now and he was forced to give in; he simply lacked the spirit to resist.

'Very well. Do what you like.'

And so it was settled. Cragg did the cooking, such as it was, but he was not in Mrs Grimble's class. He would make occasional expeditions in Reedham's car and come back with provisions and sometimes a meal of fish-and-chips. He would buy whisky too, and sometimes he would have a drinking session and become violent and break things. Reedham was afraid he might take to visiting the local pub and get drunk there. In that state there was no telling what damaging information he might let slip. But there was really no likelihood of that: Cragg himself was well aware of the danger and he avoided drawing attention to himself in public.

A woman in the village did the washing, but the housework was neglected and a general air of seediness came over the rooms, with dust and cobwebs everywhere. The gardens had long since been allowed to go back to the wild.

Sometimes Cragg would bring back a prostitute he had picked up and take her to his room. He offered to do as much for Reedham but the offer was refused.

'I'm too old for that sort of thing.'

Cragg gave a derisive laugh. 'I'm not too old and I could give you a few years.'

But as more years passed he, too, seemed to lose the urge. Perhaps he just could not be bothered to take the trouble any more. And perhaps he preferred to spend his money on whisky.

Reedham had long become accustomed to this way of life and no longer expected that any change would occur to break the dull routine until either he or Cragg became so decrepit that they had to be carted off to an old people's home – a prospect which he for his part viewed with unmitigated horror – when the painting was stolen; and that one small incident was enough to upset the entire rhythm of his existence.

* * *

That night he had been unable to sleep. Finally, after much tossing and turning, he had got up, put on a dressing-gown and gone downstairs with the object of getting himself a glass of whisky. Having reached the hall, he had heard a slight noise coming from the room on the left which served as a small picture gallery. He had opened the door of the room, switched on the light and discovered a man with a torch in his hand. The French windows were open and the cool night air had been coming in, rustling the curtains a little. All this he had noticed in a flash, and it had brought him to a halt, petrified for the moment by the shock of finding this intruder in his house.

The man had hesitated for an instant, and then he had come at him and struck him on the head with the torch. The blow had knocked him out for a while; he doubted whether it had been for more than a minute or two; and when he had regained consciousness the intruder had gone. He had not noticed the loss of the Sempler painting until he had closed the French windows and locked them.

He had not told Cragg about the incident until morning. He had bathed the cut on his temple and had put a strip of plaster on it; and of course Cragg had noticed it at once.

'Wotcher done to your napper?'

He had thought of saying that he had knocked it on a door, but sooner or later Cragg would have been bound to notice the gap where the painting had hung and would have had to be told the truth, so there would have been no point in lying.

Cragg had listened in silence to his account of the

nocturnal intrusion and it had obviously given him food for thought.

'Now why did he pick that there picture out of all the rest?'

It was a question Reedham had asked himself and had found no plausible answer. Had the thief come with the object of taking that particular painting? It seemed unlikely. So why had he taken it? Perhaps because, after having been discovered, he had been in a great hurry to escape and yet had been unwilling to depart altogether empty-handed. And so he had snatched a picture at random, and it had just happened to be that one. Perhaps. And again perhaps not.

'I don't know.'

* * *

Well, he knew now. From what this man Grant had said it was obvious that the intruder had been nothing but a petty thief, an opportunist who had found the French windows unfastened and had walked in to pick up whatever came to hand. And the irony of it was that if he, Clifford Reedham, had not interrupted him he might never have taken *Bavarian Sunset*. He would have had time to pick and choose, and would very likely have gone away with something else.

It had worried him ever since, off and on; though Cragg had dismissed the suggestion that any harm might come of it.

'So you've lost a bloody picture! So what! A bit of rubbish you'd have done better to have left where it was in the first place. No need to lose any sleep over it. It'll just be sold; somebody else will have it and that'll be that.'

Reedham had hoped so. And as the days passed, and the weeks, and there was no sign of any repercussions from the incident, he had almost come to believe that his misgivings were without foundation. And then this damned private eye had rung him up and asked him to give an interview to a client who was interested in the work of Arnold Sempler.

Then the alarm-bells had really started ringing in his head, and the visit of the three people had done nothing to silence them; especially when Miss Hoffmann had started asking questions about his war service in Europe. He wondered whether she had believed him when he had told her that he had been in the Royal Artillery and had never been to North Germany. Somehow, he doubted it.

'You worry too much,' Cragg said. 'And worryin' ain't going to make a blind bit of difference. So forget it.'

Which was easy enough to say but quite impossible to do. Reedham could not forget it, and he went on worrying in spite of Cragg's admonishment.

TEN

At Last

'At the end of winter in the last year of World War Two,' Grant said, 'the Wessex Rifles were serving in that part of Germany which is now North Rhine-Westphalia, or as you would say Nordrhein-Westfalen. They were pushing forward as part of the 21st British Army Group into Lower Saxony or Niedersachsen, moving eastward into the plains of North Germany.'

He had been doing some research into military history in his local public library, and had found no difficulty in coming up with this information.

Miss Hoffmann gave a faint sigh. It could have been of satisfaction. 'Ah!'

'In which case,' Cynara said, 'Reedham would almost certainly have been in that part of Germany.'

'If he was in fact in the Wessex Rifles and not, as he claimed, in the Royal Artillery.'

'He was lying about that, of course.'

'Probably.'

'Oh, there can be no doubt about it. I'm sure he was. But why? Why would he want to make us believe he was in quite another part of Europe at that time?'

'I've no idea.' Grant turned to Miss Hoffmann. 'Have you?'

'Yes,' she said, 'I have.'

They were all gathered again in the office of the Grant Inquiry Agency, where Gerda Hoffmann had come to hear the result of Grant's researches. The other two looked at her questioningly when she made this statement.

'And are you,' Cynara asked, 'going to tell us?'

Miss Hoffmann seemed to be thinking the matter over for a while. Then, apparently coming to a decision, she said: 'Well, perhaps I do owe you an explanation.'

'You have been keeping us rather in the dark,' Cynara said. 'And I for one am simply burning with curiosity.'

Grant was curious too, but he had no intention of putting any pressure on his client. 'There is, of course, no necessity for you to explain anything. You have a perfect right to keep things to yourself if you wish to.'

A withering glance from Cynara told him that in her opinion at least he should have kept his mouth shut. But Gerda said:

'No. I will tell you. Something happened at a schloss, a country house that is, in a part of Germany at the time when the Allied armies were rapidly advancing and the War was nearing its close.'

She stopped, as if still not sure whether it would be wise to tell more. Or possibly she was sorting things out in her mind before continuing. But soon she went on again.

'The house was almost deserted at the time. All the servants had left and there were just two people remaining: a woman and her six-year-old son. The woman's name was Wilhelmina Neuberg and the boy's name was Otto. The woman was a widow; her husband, a captain in the German army, had been killed in action on the Russian front.'

'So the house belonged to her?' Grant said.

'Yes. And the estate which went with it. Nothing had yet been seen of the Allied forces, but the woman knew that it would not be long before the advance engulfed the estate. Then one day two British soldiers arrived in a small truck, an officer and a sergeant. They appeared to be on some kind of scouting expedition and they walked into the house. The boy had seen them coming and he was present when the officer questioned his mother, but he could not understand what was being said because they spoke in English, a language he had not yet learned.'

'But which his mother could speak?'

'Yes. After a little while the officer went upstairs with the woman. The boy would have followed, but he was prevented from doing so by the sergeant, who it seems had already given a demonstration of power by firing a submachine-gun and smashing a large ceramic vase which stood in the hall. While the woman and the officer were gone the sergeant went round from room to room, helping himself to anything that took his fancy, including some medals. The boy went with him and when they returned to the hall they heard the woman screaming. The boy would have dashed up the stairs, but the sergeant seized him by the collar and again restrained him.

'A little while later the officer came down the stairs alone, dabbing at some scratches on his cheek that were bleeding. The sergeant appeared to be amused, but the officer was angry. They exchanged a few words, and then the sergeant let the boy go and he ran upstairs to his mother's bedroom. He found her unconscious on the bed, almost naked, her face bruised and bloody, as though she had been savagely beaten.'

Cynara gave a little cry: 'Oh, my God! You mean that officer had attacked her?'

Miss Hoffmann glanced at her and spoke with a kind of mocking cynicism. 'It shocks you? Why should it? In war that kind of thing is commonplace. Men become beasts. Conquering armies are expected to indulge in rape, brutality and plundering; it is the price that has to be paid for defeat. Ask any East German woman who was living at the time how the Russian soldiers behaved.'

'How do you know all this?' Grant asked. 'About the British officer and the sergeant, I mean.'

'Oh,' she said, 'it was told to me by an eye-witness.'

'An eye-witness?'

'My father. Otto Neuberg.'

'You mean the boy?'

'Yes, the boy. Now, of course, a man.'

'But your name is Hoffmann.'

'I was married to Kurt Hoffmann. I was very young at the time and he was much older. It was all a mistake; the marriage was not a success and we are now divorced.'

'And you don't wear a wedding ring,' Cynara said.

'No. It seemed ridiculous to do so in the circumstances.'

'But why tell us you were Miss Hoffmann?' Grant asked.

'I cannot recall that I ever did.'

'You didn't correct me when I called you Miss Hoffmann and introduced you to Reedham as that.'

She gave an enigmatic smile. 'It did not seem necessary. However, if you were to look at my passport you would see that it is made out in the name of Frau Hoffmann.'

'And you never told me either,' Cynara said. 'All these years and I never knew you had been married.' She sounded faintly resentful.

Gerda shrugged. 'Well, I have told you now.'

'But there is more, isn't there?' Grant said. 'You haven't yet told the whole story.'

'Ah, you are speaking about the painting. It was not discovered until a while after the two men had left that it had disappeared. No one else could have taken it, and of course it had to be the officer; the sergeant had already collected his loot.'

Grant nodded. Things were beginning to fall into place. He said: 'Is your grandmother still alive?'

'No. She died some years ago. My father lives in the schloss, but the estate is not as large as it used to be.'

'And how long has he been looking for the man who raped his mother? I take it that that is really what this is all about?'

'Yes. And you might call it his mission in life. Of course as a child he could do nothing but wait and hope. He did not know his name or what unit he had been serving in. There were no records for him to examine and all inquiries came to nothing. The one clue seemed to be the painting; if he could trace that it might lead to the man who had stolen it. But that, too, had apparently vanished.

'However, he never completely abandoned hope. He had an agreement with a German firm of art dealers by which they were to let him know if *Bavarian Sunset* by Arnold Sempler ever came up for sale, especially in a London auction. Well, the years passed and still there was nothing, no hint whatever of where the picture might be; and even he began to give up hope. Then, out of the blue, it came: the news that he had been waiting for all that time. *Bavarian Sunset* appeared in the catalogue of a forthcoming art sale by the London firm of Lingarten and Son at their Beldon Lane Auction Rooms.

' "Gerda," my father said, "you must go to London and find out who the vendor is." The name, of course was not in the catalogue.'

'Why didn't he come himself?'

'There are reasons why that was not possible.'

She did not say what the reasons were, and Grant did not ask. Maybe business affairs made it necessary for Otto Neuberg to remain in Germany for the present.

'So what happens now?'

'Now I report to him that I have found the man who assaulted my grandmother and stole the painting.'

'You feel quite certain it was Reedham?'

'Can there be any doubt now? Everything points to him.'

'That's so. But it's all circumstantial evidence. There's still no firm proof that he is your man.'

'Oh, really, Sam!' Cynara broke in. 'What further proof do you need? A signed confession? Of course it has to be him. There's no getting away from it.'

'Well, accepting that to be so,' Grant said. 'And I have to agree that it's as close to a certainty as you could get without an admission of guilt from his own lips —'

'Which we're not likely to get.'

'Which, as you say, we're not likely to get. So what, Gerda, will your father do when you tell him?'

She thought about it, and then said: 'I'm not sure he'll do anything.'

'Not do anything! Then why go to all this trouble to find the man?'

'I think perhaps in a way that's all he wanted. It's been

such a long time, you see. It's been as though the man did not exist; that it was all a kind of nightmare that had no solid basis in fact. I think he needed to know that this officer really was a thing of flesh and blood. Of course there always was the possibility that he was dead, killed maybe in the fag-end of the War. That was perhaps what my father feared most, because then he would never know the identity of the man, and that phantom from the past would never be properly exorcised.'

This all sounded rather far-fetched to Grant, and he found it difficult to swallow.

'But surely he will want to confront the man, to tax him with his crime if nothing else.'

'Perhaps. It will be for him to decide.'

Grant noticed that there was one word she had not uttered, had almost studiously avoided. Yet it was the word that had been in his own mind ever since he had heard her story. And that word was: 'Revenge'. Surely Neuberg would scarcely be human if he did not desire to inflict some retribution on Reedham for his bestial actions nearly half a century ago.

For Herr Neuberg was the boy Otto grown to manhood; the boy who had seen his mother as Reedham had left her: naked, bloody and violated. Such an experience could not but leave a lasting impression on the mind, a burning desire to get even with the man who had been responsible for the crime.

He spoke again to Gerda. 'What will you do now? Will you go back to Germany?'

'For the present I think not. I shall of course get in touch with my father.'

'Of course.' That, after all, had been the object of the exercise: to discover for Otto Neuberg the identity of the man who had raped his mother and stolen the

Arnold Sempler painting. In this exercise he, Grant, had played a part, but that was finished now, and there was nothing more for him to do than to take his fee and quietly withdraw. From this point the matter was out of his hands.

Gerda took her leave soon after that. She said she had some shopping to do. Cynara offered to accompany her, but she politely refused.

'Just for the present I think I must be on my own.'

'But I shall see you again?'

'Oh, yes; I'll keep in touch. And you know where I'm staying if you wish to contact me.'

When she had gone Cynara said: 'I don't like it.'

'What don't you like?' Grant asked.

'The feel of things.'

'You'd better explain what you mean by that.'

'Well, for a start there's this question of Otto Neuberg's motive in getting his daughter to trace Reedham. Do you believe he just wants to make sure the man exists? Or even that he'll be content simply to confront him and accuse him to his face of committing that piece of nastiness all those years ago. Be honest, Sam, do you really believe he wants nothing more than that?'

'I don't know.'

'You don't know? No, of course you don't. But put yourself in his shoes: as a boy you've practically been an eye-witness of a savage sexual assault on your mother, okay? So what are your feelings towards the man who did it? Wouldn't you want to punish him? Wouldn't you be absolutely eaten up with rage and frustration because there was nothing you could do at the time? And wouldn't you perhaps make a vow that one day you would hunt the man down and really make him pay?'

'Possibly,' Grant said. She was, of course, merely putting his own thoughts into words.

'No possibly about it. You can bet your sweet life that's what he intends to do.'

'We can't be sure of that. It was a very long time ago. He's grown up; he's had time to mellow. Even if he made a vow of revenge at the time he may no longer feel the same way about it. Memories have a tendency to fade.'

'But his memory hasn't faded; that's obvious. If it had, why would he still be hunting for the man?'

'To exorcise a ghost, as Gerda said.'

'Rubbish! I doubt whether she even believed that herself. It was just something she cooked up to head us off. My belief is that this Otto Neuberg could be a real toughie who's been storing up the memory of that injury in his mind ever since that day in 1945 when the two British soldiers walked into his mother's house. He's been nursing the grievance year after year, waiting and waiting for the time when he could really do something about it. And now that time has come. So let's not have any smooth talk about mellowing or exorcising or any of that rot. What we've got here is a case of revenge, pure and simple and very sweet; nothing more and nothing less.'

'Have you finished?' Grant asked. She had, he thought, become quite heated on the subject.

'Yes, I've finished. But I don't think he has. Now do you agree with me or don't you?'

'I think you have a point.'

'Darn right, I have. So what are you going to do about it?'

'Me! What is there I can do?'

'You could go to the police.'

'And tell them what? That I have a feeling that a certain German is coming to England to take revenge on a certain Englishman for an incident that occurred at the end of World War Two in Lower Saxony? They'd laugh at me.'

'It would be up to you to convince them that you were telling the truth. That Mr Reedham is in grave danger.'

'Well, even if I could – which I very much doubt – what could they do? Give Reedham round-the-clock protection? He hasn't even asked for it, and I'm pretty certain he wouldn't get it if he did.'

'They could make a check at the airports and so on to see if Neuberg slipped into the country.'

'And if he did, what then? They couldn't keep him out, because as far as we know he's done nothing wrong. All they'd have to go on would be a vague suspicion thrown up by a private investigator that he might be planning to commit a crime. A bit thin, wouldn't you say?'

She frowned. She was reluctant to admit that it was, but she could hardly deny the fact.

'There must be something we can do.'

'Why are you so concerned? Do you think Reedham is worth bothering about? Don't you think he deserves anything that may be coming to him?'

'Yes, but –'

'It's not our pigeon, Cynara. Leave it.'

She said nothing more, but he could see that she was unhappy about it. And if it came to the point, he was none too happy himself.

*   *   *

Gerda Hoffmann had not in fact gone shopping.

Instead, she had put through a telephone call to Germany and had a brief conversation with the person at the other end of the line. The person was a man and his name was Otto Neuberg. He seemed greatly pleased with what his daughter had to tell him.

'At last!' he said. 'At last!'

ELEVEN

Otto

In a large room in the Neuberg schloss in Lower Saxony
a number of men were gathered. They were mostly
young, many with close-cropped heads, leather-belted
and with brown shirts bearing swastika insignia on the
sleeves. The air was thick with tobacco smoke, and the
men were sitting at tables on which were big mugs of
beer.

The room was chiefly remarkable for the way it was
furnished: the walls were draped with banners like
those which had once been borne aloft at Nazi rallies in
Nuremberg in the 1930s; rallies at which the Fuehrer
would make his rabble-rousing speeches and receive the
homage of thousands of outstretched arms and cries of
'Heil Hitler!'.

And here in this room it was almost as though the
man himself were present; for at one end above a raised
dais was a life-size portrait of him; the limp forelock, the
Charlie Chaplin moustache, the staring madman's eyes,
Iron Cross on chest, one hand on belt, the other thrust
out in the Nazi salute. In the subdued lighting, which
seemed to add to the theatricality of the setting, the
portrait appeared to take on an extra dimension, to

become genuine flesh and blood; the hero summoned back from the grave to receive the adulation and worship of these followers of a later generation.

This was a gathering of neo-Nazis, the majority too young even to be able to remember the War, but a few veterans with memories of the good times when the Party had been all-powerful in Germany, when the Fatherland was pushing its borders further to the east and the promise was that the Third Reich would last a thousand years. Well, it had not done that, but Naziism was not yet dead; it would rise once more. It had grown from small beginnings in the first place and why should it not do the same again? Already young people were coming in; soon the tide would begin to flow. They drank their beer, sucked their pipes and enjoyed their dreams.

There were cheers when Otto Neuberg climbed on to the dais to address the gathering. He was a lean, rather gaunt-looking man in his middle fifties, with a scarred face and greying hair. His voice was harsh, and he spoke with a kind of suppressed anger, as if he bore a grudge against some person or persons who were not there to hear his words.

There was nothing new in his speech; most of it the audience had heard before, but they had no objection to hearing it again. He told them that their time was coming; that they were the spearhead of a movement that could not be stopped. Already, he said, their fellow Nazis to the east were taking action to drive out foreign workers who were taking jobs from native Germans. 'Why,' he demanded, 'should we allow Turks and Negroes to batten on our country and suck the life-blood of our people? Send them back where they belong. We do not want them here.'

He continued in this vein for some time, interrupted now and then by shouts of agreement and cheering from the audience. They all loved it. It was what they wanted to hear. He spoke bitterly and angrily, harping on the grievances they all nursed in their hearts and rousing their worst passions and petty hatreds.

Once, on his invitation, an Englishman had come to address them. The Englishman had not been alive at the time when the Nazis had been in power, but he had written books which contradicted generally accepted views regarding that evil regime. He had told them that they had no reason to feel ashamed of what Hitler had done; the Fuehrer had been a great man, a true Germanic hero, undeservedly maligned by his enemies. He had told them that the gas-chambers and the death-camps were a myth invented by the Jews; that there had never been a holocaust, and that the Nuremberg trials of so-called war criminals had been a farce.

Secretly Neuberg despised this man, but he was a useful tool; an outsider who gave his support to what the neo-Nazis preached. That was the only reason why he had been invited there.

At the end of his address on the present occasion Neuberg made an announcement: he was about to depart on a secret mission. He did not say what the mission was, but he seemed to hint that it was of great importance, and perhaps not without some danger to himself. The impression given was that it was in some way connected with the neo-Nazi movement, though he did not specifically state this. In conclusion he invited his hearers to wish him success. He gave the Nazi salute and shouted:

'Heil Hitler!'

They rose to their feet and answered the salute. 'Heil Hitler! Heil Hitler!'

He allowed himself a faint grim smile before turning smartly and quitting the dais. It had all been most encouraging.

*   *   *

Otto Neuberg's whole life had been overshadowed by that wartime incident at the schloss in Lower Saxony. He grew up with a burning hatred of all things British, and especially of the man who had committed the crime for which there could never be any forgiveness from him. He never forgot the vow he had made at the time, the vow to kill the man. Even when it had seemed impossible that the killing would ever be carried out he had not lost hope. Some day the hour would come and the execution would be carried out.

As a young man he entered a famous old university with the object of studying economics, but he was never a diligent student; he was more interested in politics and was appalled by what he regarded as the betrayal of his country by the new men in government. The establishment of the European Economic Community was seen by him to be embracing the enemy, and the only consolation was that Britain was not a member.

Instead of applying himself to his studies he engaged in activities that would probably have been frowned upon by the authorities if they had not been kept secret. He joined a group of like-minded fellow students whose avowed object was to keep alive the militaristic traditions of the old Germany. Not that they were able to do anything very effective in this line; it was mainly a charade; but they held meetings in an old beer cellar and sang martial songs and inflicted sabre wounds on one another's cheeks as badges of manhood.

Eventually these activities could no longer be kept secret; the information reached the ears of the university authorities who felt it incumbent upon them to take strict action. As a consequence, some of the ringleaders were expelled, and chief among these was Otto Neuberg.

When he arrived back at the family home his mother was more shocked by the scars on his face than the act of his expulsion. She had not remarried and was managing what remained of the estate on her own. A few of the old retainers had returned, and the house was more inviting than it had been in that winter of 1945.

There was in fact no shortage of money. Otto's grandfather had been a wealthy man and had had the foresight to invest a quantity of his wealth in Switzerland and Sweden. He had perhaps foreseen that another war was coming and that once again Germany might be defeated, rendering the Deutsche Mark worthless. He had not lived to see this come true, but his prudence was to ensure that his daughter-in-law and grandson were not ruined by World War Two as so many others were. In fact, they were quite well off, and there was no necessity for Otto to seek a job if he did not wish to do so. And he had no such wish; he much preferred to live the life of a country gentleman and take over from his mother the responsibility of managing the estate.

At the age of twenty-five he married Johanna Riegler, an Austrian girl whom he had met while on a visit to Vienna. She was lovely; for a while she made him so happy that he almost forgot his disgust with the way Germany was going, snuggling up to former enemies and forgetting its own glorious past; and even that vow to find and kill the Englishman who had violated his mother was forced temporarily into the background. Then the child was born, the daughter whom they named Gerda, and life was good.

But all too soon tragedy was to strike. Johanna, out riding, was thrown from her horse, broke her neck and died. And some weeks later his mother took an overdose of sleeping-pills, whether purposely or by accident no one could say. It happened to be the anniversary of the day when she had been raped. This could have been a coincidence, but Otto Neuberg refused to believe that it was; and now, what with this and the loss of his wife, all the bitterness returned, and not even the childish prattling of his golden-haired daughter could dispel it. In his mind he somehow managed to link the deaths of both women to that inhuman monster who had crossed his path once in life, and whom he would strain every nerve and sinew to run to earth and kill.

*   *   *

He engaged a nurse to look after the child and later she was sent away to a school in Switzerland, so that for long periods he saw nothing of her. He was by now deeply involved in the neo-Nazi movement and using his money to further the cause. He did not really believe that Nazis would ever again take power in Germany, but he was so bitterly opposed to the existing government and all its works that he would have done anything to embarrass it.

In one attempt to trace the man he was looking for he paid a visit to England. He had learned the language so that when the time came he would be able to speak to the man in his own tongue, and this was an advantage now. But he could get no lead: the military records he was able to examine told him nothing beyond the fact that there had indeed been British forces operating in the vicinity of his home at the time when the incident had taken place. But without any knowledge of the names or units of the two men who had come to the schloss, it was impossible to trace them. He felt, too, that the authorities were being deliberately obstructive when they became aware of what he was looking for. In a case such as this the honour of a famous regiment might be at stake, and the last thing they would have desired would have been bad publicity.

So he found himself up against a brick wall; but while he was in London he made contact with a number of like-minded people; members of an extreme right-wing group which had broken away from the National Front because it was considered to be insufficiently aggressive in its activities. He was welcomed with open arms as one of their own kind, and he was assured that they revered the late Adolf Hitler as a great hero, a shining example to later generations. He was told that a demonstration in Trafalgar Square was being planned and he was invited to take part.

He accepted with alacrity. The truth was that he had no liking for these activists, who in his opinion were mainly uncouth, ignorant hooligans; but their enemy, the British Establishment, was his enemy, and he was prepared in any way he could to strike a blow for those who were doing their utmost to cause it as much nuisance as possible.

The demonstration was illegal, and the demonstrators were, as indeed they had expected, attacked by left-wingers. The whole affair developed into a riot; the police moved in in force and a number of arrests were made. One of those arrested was Otto Neuberg. He appeared in court on a charge of taking part in an affray and was ordered to be deported and declared persona non grata in the United Kingdom.

* * *

Gerda had been told nothing about her grandmother's ordeal until she was quite grown up. Then one day her father summoned her to his study.

'There is something,' he said, 'which I think it is time you should know. It is not right that you should remain in ignorance of it any longer.'

He motioned to her to sit down, which she did in one of the leather-upholstered armchairs; but he remained standing, one arm resting on the mantelpiece above the large open fireplace.

'It concerns your grandmother.'

The gravity with which he spoke was enough to warn her that what she was about to hear would not be anything of a pleasant nature. But she could not for a moment have guessed what it was, and she felt a deep sense of shock when the revelation was made. It was almost like a physical thing, as if she herself were suffering that indignity, that violation, that sexual assault on her body.

'All those years,' she murmured. 'Living with the memory of that. All those years.' It made her sick to think of it. Indignant too.

Neuberg was watching her, noting her reaction to the story. He could tell that it had affected her acutely. That was as it should be. He would have been disappointed if she had received the information calmly, without emotion, as something that had taken place too long ago to have any impact on her feelings now.

'I see that you are moved by this story,' he said.

She stared at him, wide-eyed. 'Did you expect anything else? Who would not be?'

'Such things happened to many German women in those days. It became too common to be remarked.'

She knew that this was true, but it made no difference. What happened to a thousand other women could perhaps be accepted as commonplace, but when it came close to you, into your own family, it ceased to be in the ordinary run of things and became exceptional.

'That man,' she said. 'What a monster he must have been.'

'And yet he looked quite unremarkable.'

'Ah!' she said. 'You saw him, of course.' She had almost overlooked the fact that her father had been there; a boy, and witness to such horror. 'How you must have suffered!'

'Suffered! I?' It seemed to be quite a new thought to him. It was not his suffering that he remembered; it was his anger; the consuming desire for revenge. 'No, it was she who suffered. I hated him for what he had done to her. You cannot imagine the hatred I felt in my heart. It has never died. That is why I have continued searching for him, year after year. I cannot rest until I meet him again face to face, confront him, accuse him.'

'But suppose he is dead?'

'Then I shall have been robbed. But no; I cannot believe he is dead. He must not be. I have to see him, speak to him. It is what I live for; that day.'

He did not tell her of the vow he had made; that he would kill the man. He was not sure enough of her to confide in her to that extent. She might have reservations about helping him in his search if she was aware of the eventual purpose of it. And he might need her help; she was an intelligent girl and he could depend on her to carry out any instructions he might give.

They had never been particularly close, he and Gerda. Perhaps it had been his fault. He wondered whether she loved him; he had never asked and she had never expressed any feelings of affection for him. Did she respect him, even? He could not be sure.

He was not at all certain that she approved of that connection with the neo-Nazis, though she had never uttered any word of criticism regarding it. He had never ventured to ask her what her views were concerning the European Community. She was young, and generally speaking it appeared that the younger generation, the majority of them at least, were greatly in favour of closer links between the countries of Europe; it was their kind of vision – one big happy family of nations. They were misguided of course, but that was the way of things. And so he did not dare to ask his daughter whether she believed in the goals towards which certain politicians were urging the Community, for the simple reason that he feared what the answer might be.

And Gerda herself had never offered her opinion on the matter. In that respect, as in certain others, she remained an enigma to him.

* * *

That evening when Otto Neuberg addressed the gathering in the Adolf Hitler room at his home in Lower Saxony he was feeling particularly elated. The reason for this elation was that earlier in the day he had received a telephone call from his daughter, who was speaking from London. The conversation had been brief but to the point.

'I have found him,' Gerda said.

Neuberg did not ask whom she had found. He knew that she was referring to the man he had been seeking for half a century. He gave a long sigh of satisfaction.

'At last! At last!'

He did not ask to be told the man's name; it was not important. Nor did he ask for any details regarding the search; all that he would be able to hear later.

'What do you wish me to do now?' Gerda asked.

'Remain where you are. I will send instructions. Meanwhile, you must rent a car. You will have some driving to do.'

'Very well.'

'That is all.'

No word of love. No word of congratulation. Merely a cool acceptance of what she had succeeded in doing. Well, that was the way of things between them; in their relations with each other there had never been any suggestion of emotion.

She wondered how he would have reacted if she had told how much she had revealed to Grant and Cynara. She had a feeling that he would not have been pleased, that in fact he might have been deeply angered. She half regretted that she had told them so much; it had not been necessary. But somehow she had felt a need to confide in someone, and she had felt sure that they would listen with sympathy and respect her confidence.

Nevertheless, perhaps it had been a mistake.

* * *

Otto Neuberg himself had one confidant: a man named Karl Schroeder, in whom he had complete trust. Schroeder was sixty years old and had been in the Hitler Youth movement. In the closing days of the War he had in fact carried arms, though he was still only a boy. He had been a fanatical disciple of the Fuehrer then and had remained a fantatic ever since. His dearest memory was of having received a pat on the head from Hitler himself, together with a word or two of praise. He would have died for his leader, and in fact came very near to doing so when a Russian bullet passed through his right arm. Later he was taken away to Russia as a prisoner-of-war and proved his toughness by surviving the harsh conditions and being one of those who eventually made it back to Germany.

Neuberg had come across this stocky, hard-faced, bullet-headed man in the neo-Nazi group, and had picked him out as one who might be useful to have at his disposal. He had offered to employ him as a kind handyman with no specific duties; and Schroeder, who had never held a steady job in his life, had accepted the offer without hesitation.

It was Karl Schroeder, therefore, who was the only person present that evening to be aware of what the secret mission was, on which Neuberg had stated that he was about to depart. Schroeder knew all about it, and was in fact to accompany Neuberg; but he told no one. When entrusted with a secret, torture would not have extracted the information from him. Neuberg knew this, and it was the utter trustworthiness of the man that was one of the qualities which had made him such a valued retainer.

After receiving the telephone call Neuberg summoned Schroeder to his study and told him what was afoot.

'My daughter has located the man I told you about.'

Schroeder's pale blue eyes seemed to glow faintly. 'The Englishman?'

'Yes, the Englishman.'

'And you will be going to see him?'

'I shall be going to see him and you will accompany me.'

Schroeder showed no surprise at this; it was no more than he would have expected. He did not ask what Neuberg would say to the Englishman or what he would do. There was an understanding between the two men, and Schroeder had come to accept that Neuberg's quarrel was his quarrel also; that his master's enemy was his enemy.

'When do we leave?'

'There will be arrangements to make. As soon as possible. You will be ready?'

'I am always ready,' Schroeder said.

TWELVE

No Autobahn

It was almost a week since she had made the telephone call to her father when Gerda received a letter with a German stamp on it. She had spent a good deal of her time in the company of Cynara. Miss Jones acted as a guide to London; they saw the sights, visited art galleries and museums, went to the theatre, and the days passed very pleasantly.

Gerda had got herself a car from a rental firm as instructed by Neuberg, but she had as yet used it very little; it stayed for the most part in the basement garage at the hotel. She had credit cards and her German driver's licence, and there had been no difficulty with the formalities of renting.

When she saw the envelope waiting for her at the reception desk she had a feeling that this period of pleasant relaxation was coming to an end. She took the envelope to her room where she could open it in private, and inside she discovered the briefest of notes, together with a map. The note contained instructions as to what she was to do. The map was a large-scale one of North Norfolk, and a certain point on the coast was marked with a cross. There was also a date.

Having read the note and examined the map, she refolded both and put them back in the envelope, which she then stowed away in her handbag. When she had done this she returned to the reception desk and informed the clerk that she would be leaving next morning, but that she wished to reserve her room, since she would be back again within a few days. She also wished to reserve two more rooms if any were available. She was assured that there were and she made the reservation.

In the morning she checked out, took the rented car, a Ford Sierra, from the hotel garage and drove it to Norwich. This was all strange country to her, but she had little difficulty in finding the way once she had got herself on to the A 11. She had never previously been to Norwich, but she had no time to spend sightseeing in that ancient city at this time; there were more important matters calling for her attention. She had arrived soon after midday, and having taken a light lunch she reclaimed her Sierra from the high-rise car park where she had left it and drove northward to the coast.

The summer season was over and finding accommodation presented no problem. She settled for a motel chalet at one of the holiday resorts and made this her temporary base for operations. There was still time left to make a trip eastward along the coast to a small village which was marked on the map her father had sent her, and this she did. The village was separated from the sea by marshes, and a narrow road gave access to a shingly beach some half a mile or so away.

Gerda drove as far as the beach and parked the Sierra. There were some huts lined up on a bank above the high-tide mark, but nobody seemed to be using them at the moment. She climbed the bank and found the beach deserted apart from a few hardy fishermen, well wrapped-up against the chilly breeze, and a man walking a dog. It was a dull cloudy afternoon, and the sea looked grey and uninviting. It was not rough, but the waves made a continual low thunder as they broke on the shore and then retreated, dragging the shingle with them with a rushing scurrying sound.

She did not stay long; she had seen all she needed to see and knew just where she had to come later. She returned to the car and drove away.

She spent the evening in her chalet, watching television until eleven o'clock. Then she dressed herself warmly in jeans, a shirt, a thick woollen jumper and a quilted anorak, left the chalet and took her car from the motel park.

It was not yet midnight when she reached the place which she had reconnoitred some hours earlier. She stopped the car, switched off the lights and got out. It was a cold night, the sky overcast and a dampness in the air which did not quite amount to a drizzle. With the aid of a small pocket torch she found her way up the bank and on to the beach, passing between the silent huts. She came to a halt and gazed out across the sea. But nothing was visible in the darkness, and when she had switched off the tiny light of the pocket torch there was only the glimmer of the surf where the waves were breaking to give a hint of whiteness in the gloom.

She prepared herself to wait. It might be for hours. Her father had given no definite time of arrival. How could he? There were so many factors to be taken into account, so many imponderables that could affect the timing. Was it even certain that he would arrive that night?

The hours passed slowly. She walked back and forth

along the beach, made nervous by the sound of her own footsteps, imagining that someone was following and turning suddenly to make sure that no one was there. There was a wind coming off the sea, not strong but penetrating; in spite of her thick clothing she felt chilled to the bone. She went back to the car and sat in it for a while, drinking hot coffee from a flask she had brought. Perhaps it would be all right if she waited for him there; surely he would find his way to the road. But she could not be sure of it; she ought to be on the beach keeping a lookout; and after a while she returned to her lonely vigil.

It had begun to grow light when she finally gave up. In the distance a faint greyness was spreading over the sea, but nothing was visible out there. He would not come now; she could be sure of that. She drove back to the chalet and went to bed.

*　*　*

He came the next night, and there was another man with him. They landed on the beach from an inflatable boat with an outboard motor. Somewhere out to sea was a small fishing vessel from which the boat had come and to which it would return as soon as the two passengers had been disembarked. It was two o'clock in the morning and a light rain was falling. The men were carrying suitcases.

Gerda had been waiting since before midnight, and she had begun to fear that it might again be a fruitless vigil. She was cold and wet and low in spirits; and though the arrival of her father brought a sense of relief, she felt no great elation. And all Neuberg said by way of greeting was a brief:

'Ah! So you are here!'

He did not embrace her. She had not expected him to. But there was a kind of flatness about it all; the note was subdued.

'This is Karl.' Neuberg indicated the other man.

But for the darkness she would have recognised him at once. She knew Schroeder and disliked him. She had known that her father would be bringing a companion; he had indicated as much in his letter; but he had not said who it would be. The choice of Schroeder was not one that Gerda would have desired; it had a depressing effect on her. She had a feeling of disquiet, almost of dread. But she said nothing.

Schroeder was silent as they walked to the car. She opened the boot and they stowed the suitcases inside. Neuberg got into the front passenger seat and Schroeder rode in the back. She started the car and drove it away from the beach and on to the coastal road, the windscreen wipers sweeping the glass and raindrops pattering on the roof.

'I was here yesterday,' she said. 'I waited all night on the beach.'

'It was not possible to get here then. The damned boat had engine trouble,' Neuberg said. He spoke complainingly, with no hint of apology, no suggestion of any sympathy for her. It was as though he took it for granted that she would be happy enough to wait on a cold and lonely beach for as long as it might take, and that the only inconvenience that mattered had been to him.

They came to the motel. She drove the car on to the park and they all got out. She thought the men might leave their suitcases in the car, but apparently Neuberg was unwilling to take the risk of having them stolen. So she unlocked the boot and they took their luggage, following her to the chalet. There was not a sign of anyone else moving around at that time of night, and they went inside and she switched on the light.

The men put their suitcases down and took off their wet coats, while Gerda discarded her anorak. She had drawn the curtains before leaving, and no one could have seen in. She doubted, too, whether anyone had seen them arrive. Not that it mattered; it might have seemed odd perhaps, but who would have bothered? From their appearance there was nothing to proclaim the fact that the two men had entered the country illegally.

The chalet had a bedroom, a sitting-room, a bathroom and a small kitchen for self-catering. The furnishing was plain but adequate. Neuberg cast a glance round the accommodation and gave a nod of approval.

'Satisfactory?' Gerda asked. There was a faint note of sarcasm in the question.

Apparently oblivious to the slight teasing, he answered curtly: 'It will do.'

'It will have to, won't it? Did you have a good crossing?'

'No. As I said, the engine broke down. There was a possibility that we might have to send out a distress signal, and that would have ruined everything.' He spoke testily, as if blaming the engine for deliberately making trouble for him, and the crew of the vessel for allowing it to do so. 'They are scum, those seamen; the skipper as bad as any. A damned crook.'

'Perhaps if they were not crooks and scum they might not be doing such jobs. Where did you sail from?'

'Bremerhaven.'

She was not surprised. It was in Lower Saxony, and from there she supposed the voyage would have taken only two or three days in the absence of any engine failure. She wondered how much it would cost. Quite a lot, no doubt; people who did jobs of that sort expected to be well paid for their trouble. But her father would not have let the cost deter him; he was, one might have said, on the way to fulfilling his life's ambition, and nothing could be allowed to stand in his path.

'Are you hungry?' she asked. 'I brought some canned stuff, and I could cook something. Or would you like a hot drink now and breakfast before we leave in the morning?'

He settled for that. Schroeder was not consulted and he did not offer any suggestions.

Gerda went into the kitchen and made three cups of coffee. When she had drunk hers she took a hot shower in the bathroom and then went to bed for the few hours left of the night. She had a long drive ahead of her and needed rest.

* * *

She was roused from a deep sleep by someone shaking her with a hand on her shoulder. It was her father.

'Come,' he said. 'It is time you were up and about. We don't want to waste time here.'

It was in fact seven o'clock; she had had less than four hours of sleep and felt she could have used a lot more. But she could tell that Neuberg was eager to be on the move; not because there was really any need for haste but because he could not bear to hang around; he needed to get closer to that meeting with Clifford Reedham; he could hardly wait to see him face to face.

In the event they did not have breakfast in the chalet. Neuberg suggested instead that they should stop at some place on the way, and his suggestions were the equivalent of decisions; he invited no argument. So Gerda packed her bag and returned the key to the office. The woman at the desk appeared surprised that she was leaving so soon.

'I thought you intended staying longer.'

'Something came up,' Gerda said.

The woman nodded. 'That's the way it goes.'

A bizarre idea flashed into Gerda's mind. What if she were to tell this woman that the something comprised two Germans landed on a nearby beach in the middle of the night, and that one of them was going to confront the man who raped his mother fifty years ago. What would she say to that? Probably she would not believe it, would think it was some crazy joke. But it was no joke; it was very far from that; it might even be a tragedy in the making. The thought sent a shudder down her spine, and the woman noticed.

'Are you cold?'

'A little.'

'It's a chilly morning. But you'll be warm enough in your car with the heater on.'

'Yes, I'll be warm enough then.'

* * *

They had breakfast at a Little Chef café. Neuberg seemed to have little appetite, but Schroeder ate like a hog: fried eggs, bacon, sausage; he shovelled them all down as though he had not eaten for days. Gerda observed him with disdain; he was a brute, coarse and vulgar; probably vicious too. But he was a survivor; he had survived the defeat of Germany, the long march into Russia and the bitter hardship of the Siberian prison camp. You had to be tough, both mentally and physically, to come through all that and still be alive to tell the tale.

'How much farther is it to London?' Neuberg asked.

'About one hundred and eighty kilometres,' Gerda said.

'And no autobahn?'

'No autobahn.'

'A backward country,' Schroeder said, sneeringly.

'They won the War.' Gerda spoke sharply. 'You Nazis lost. Don't forget that.'

Schroeder's slablike face reddened with anger. 'We did not lose to the English; it was the Americans and the Russians. They ganged up against us. Another time it will be different.'

'There will not be another time. All that madness is finished.'

'You think so? Wait and see.'

Gerda was about to answer sharply again. She had become angered by this oaf and felt an urge to put him in his place. But Neuberg broke in.

'Stop it. This is no time for pointless argument. Let us finish our breakfast and be on our way.'

Gerda shrugged. He was right about the pointlessness of arguing with a creature like Karl Schroeder, who had a closed mind. She felt annoyed with herself for letting his remark get under her skin; she should have ignored it; it had been demeaning to bandy words with him.

As for Schroeder, he returned to his food with apparently increased appetite and a knowing smile which incensed the girl. She could not understand how her father could tolerate such a henchman.

*   *   *

They reached London in the early afternoon and checked in at the hotel. Neuberg had waited until this moment for a full account of how Gerda had succeeded in running Clifford Reedham to earth. Now he summoned her to his room to tell the whole story. Schroeder was also present, since there were to be no secrets from him, and he was already well acquainted with the history of the wartime incident at the Neuberg schloss.

'So now, Gerda,' Neuberg said, 'let us hear just how you managed to trace this Mr Reedham. Did you have much difficulty?'

'Some difficulty, certainly,' she admitted. 'And I don't think I could have done it if I had not had help.'

'Help?' Neuberg appeared startled. It was evident that he had not suspected that she had had any assistance, and it did not altogether please him to learn that she had. 'You mean there was someone aiding you in this search?'

'Yes. Two people in fact. Cynara Jones, an old friend whom I met some years ago in Austria, and a man named Sam Grant she introduced to me. He is a private investigator.'

Neuberg frowned. He seemed less and less to like what he was hearing. 'Are you telling me you engaged a private detective to trace this man? Had you taken leave of your senses?'

'Not at all. It was the only way. I had come to a dead end, you see.'

'I do not see. But you had better tell me all.'

She did so, explaining how it was that Grant could gain information that she could not have hoped to get for herself. 'He knows people, criminals and the like. It's part of his job.' She described how they had finally had an interview with Reedham, who had told them he had bought the picture in an antiques shop, and that he had never been in North Germany at the end of the War, although he had been in the British Army. 'But Sam did some research which proved he was lying. He had in fact been with a unit that was in the right place at the right time. So everything pointed to him and there could no longer be any reasonable doubt that he was your man.'

'You are quite convinced of that?'

'Yes.'

Neuberg was silent for a while; he seemed to be thinking over what she had told him. Then he said: 'This Sam Grant sounds like a very clever investigator. I hope you did not tell him why you wanted to trace the owner of the picture. Did you?'

Gerda had been expecting this question and was ready with a lie: 'Of course not. Did you suppose I would?'

'I could hardly imagine you would be so foolish. But a man like that – and the girl – would no doubt have been curious, I imagine.'

'Oh yes, they were curious.'

'And asked questions?'

'Yes.'

'But you told them nothing?'

'I told them simply that I was making a study of the works of Arnold Sempler and wished to trace the vendor of a painting called *Bavarian Sunset*, which had recently been sold by auction in London. Just for purposes of my research.'

'And that satisfied them?'

'I don't think it did. But they had to accept it.'

Neuberg gave her a searching look, and she guessed that he was wondering whether to believe her. Perhaps she had been just a shade too glib. Maybe what she had told him sounded like something carefully prepared to hide the truth of the matter.

But he did not press her further, and went on to ask about the meeting with Clifford Reedham at Marley Hall. He insisted on being told everything that had been said; he wanted a full description of Reedham's appearance and the manner in which he had reacted to the questioning.

'Did he appear nervous?'

She thought about that; and then: 'A little, perhaps; though he covered it very well. It was when I suddenly asked him whether he had been in the army during the War that he seemed to be thrown off balance for a moment. But he recovered quickly, and I knew he could see what I was aiming at. And then when I suggested he might have taken part in the advance into North Germany he said he had never touched that section of the front. His story was that he had been in the Royal Artillery, but Sam spotted a photograph of him in a group of men of the Wessex Rifles, which did see action in Nordrhein-Westfalen. So why would he lie about it if he didn't have a guilty conscience regarding his actions at that time? And besides, the coincidence that he later picked up in a shop in England the very picture that had been stolen from your house at that very time is quite impossible to believe.'

'Yes,' Neuberg said. 'Everything points to him. He has to be the man. Who else is with him at this Marley Hall? A wife? Servants?'

'He is not married and he is being looked after by just

one employee, a man named Cragg, an elderly rough-looking person. He told us he could get no one else. The place looks very neglected.'

Neuberg was silent for a time, evidently giving some deep thought to the matter. Both Gerda and Schroeder watched him, waiting for him to come to some decision. Finally he said:

'How far is this Marley Hall from here?'

'About twenty miles – thirty kilometres, say.'

'That is not far. How long would it take to get there?'

'It would depend on the state of the London traffic. It could be done in an hour or so if there were no bad hold-ups.'

Again Neuberg seemed to be mulling over the information given him, stroking his chin reflectively. Then he came to a decision.

'We could go out there today, but I think it might be better if we were to take a night's rest first. You, Gerda, have had a long drive and we are all a little tired. Tomorrow we shall be freshened up and ready for anything.'

He did not ask for the opinion of the other two; they were subordinates who could be expected to carry out his orders without question. Gerda was aware of this attitude on his part and could not avoid a feeling of resentment. She felt that he took too much for granted. Without her assistance he would probably never have traced Clifford Reedham; and who else would have met him on the beach at dead of night? Yet he had shown no appreciation of what she had done; he had simply accepted it as something to be expected from her.

And now he was making the decisions and consulting no one. He could at least have asked if she agreed with him, even if it was immaterial whether she did or not.

The fact was, he was still treating her as a child over whom he had complete authority. And she did not like it.

Karl Schroeder made no comment. It made no difference to him whether they went now or later.

THIRTEEN

Good Guns

Gerda did not sleep well. She had bad dreams. In one of
them they were all at Marley Hall, and her father and
Schroeder were torturing Clifford Reedham. She
wanted to stop them but was unable to do so. Schroeder
held Reedham while Neuberg seized his right arm and
wrenched it out of its socket. Blood spouted from the
shoulder and Reedham was screaming. Gerda screamed
also and woke shivering.

She feared to sleep again, but dozed off and had a
return of the nightmare; worse this time. Her father
and Schroeder were bludgeoning Reedham; he was on
the floor and his head was being smashed to a bloody
pulp. Again she screamed and woke in terror, bathed in
perspiration.

Looking at her watch, she saw that it was coming up to
four o'clock. she got up and went to the bathroom and
ran the bath. She got into it and lay soaking for nearly
an hour. Then she dried herself, put on a towelling
bathrobe and lay on the bed with her eyes open and the
light on, thinking.

She felt trapped. And the trap was one into which she
had walked voluntarily, not realising the full import of

her action. Now she was well and truly in and could sense the bars closing round her ever more closely, and she wondered how she could break out. Was it yet too late?

But perhaps she was exaggerating things in her mind. Dreams were only dreams, not reality. In the event no harm might come of this business; it could be as she had said to Grant and Cynara, that her father merely wished to confront the man. Could there be anything wrong in that? Yes, but in that case why had he brought Karl Schroeder with him? For company perhaps? Yes, that had to be the reason; there was nothing sinister in taking a manservant with you when you were going on a journey. Was there? Even if this was no ordinary journey.

The thoughts went round in her head like mice in a cage, swaying her first one way and then the other. She just did not know what to believe. She wished she had never had anything to do with the affair. She wished she had never enlisted the help of Cynara.

* * *

At seven o'clock she heard a knock on the door. She got off the bed and opened it to discover her father there, shaved and dressed.

'So you are awake,' he said. 'Good. Get dressed and come to my room. I wish to talk to you.'

He did not say what he wished to talk about and she did not ask; she would find out soon enough. He went away, leaving her to dress. She did so quickly and went to his room and tapped on the door. It opened a few inches and her father peered out.

'Ah, it's you. Come inside.'

He opened the door wide enough for her to enter, then closed it again and locked it. She thought he was being very cautious, but then she glanced at the bed and saw the reason why. There was a canvas cloth spread on the coverlet, and on it was a self-loading pistol and a box of cartridges. Schroeder was standing by the bed, and he had another pistol in his hand and a cleaning-rag. He grinned at her, showing his discoloured uneven teeth, amused by her reaction to the sight of the weapons.

So they had brought guns with them; she had not been aware of that until now. And why would they want to go to Marley Hall armed if it was merely to be a peaceable meeting?

Neuberg said: 'We shall be going this evening. I thought you should know.'

'Why so late in the day?'

'It is better that some things are done after dark.'

His words had an ominous sound. She glanced at the weapons. 'Are you taking those?'

'Naturally.'

'Why?'

'As a precaution.'

She did not believe him. She was certain now that what he had in mind was far more than a simple meeting with Reedham, an accusation face to face. That would not be enough to satisfy him; not nearly enough.

'You mean to kill him.' It was not a question but a statement of fact. She knew.

He shrugged. 'We shall see.'

The full enormity of his intentions came home to her now; there was no longer any possibility of mental evasion. He intended killing Reedham and she would be an accessory to the murder. She was horrified. She could not let it happen. She had to prevent it somehow.

But how? What could she do?

Suppose she were to refuse to take him to Marley Hall? The possibility entered her head and was dismissed. He would force her to do it; with a gun in her side if necessary. He was ruthless enough, and he had Schroeder to help him. And besides, even if she did not take them, they would get to Marley Hall by other means; she had shown them where it was on the road map.

Should she go to the police? It was still not too late for that. But what would she tell them? That she had knowledge of an impending murder? Would they believe her? And besides, could she betray her own father in that way, little as she might love him? It was unthinkable.

She wondered how she could have been so blind as not to foresee what the inevitable consequence of success would be when she had been searching for the man who had taken the Sempler painting. She should have done so, and it would have been easy to pull out then. But somehow there had been a sense of unreality about the whole thing; it had been a kind of game, a puzzle: find the man. And she had become absorbed in it, without stopping to think where it was all leading. So she had gone on and on until this critical point had been reached and she found herself inextricably involved in a plan to carry out a cold-blooded murder.

Schroeder had put down the pistol he had been cleaning and was now engaged in filling a magazine with ammunition. The pistols were both Walthers of nine millimetre calibre, the clips holding eight rounds each. Plenty to kill a man.

She watched Schroeder, repelled yet fascinated by the slow, deliberate motion of his fingers. He noticed her looking at him and grinned again.

'Good guns. German. Best in the world.'

She had no desire to know that. It gave her no feeling of patriotic pride. The world would surely have been a better place to live in if guns had never been invented. They were simply implements of destruction; the tools of madmen and murderers. And there was Schroeder handling them as if he loved them. But Schroeder was a brute, an animal, or worse.

She said: 'Why do you have to kill him?'

Neuberg said: 'I made a vow. I was six years old and I made a vow to take revenge.'

'But that was all so long ago.'

'All the more reason for carrying out the vow. He has escaped justice for too long.'

'Is it justice to take the law into your own hands? Execution without trial.'

'A man like that deserves no trial. Do you still not realise what he did? Don't you have any feeling about that? She was your grandmother. Have you forgotten that?'

'Of course I haven't forgotten, and of course I have feelings. But it all happened so far in the past. He is an old man now.'

'Age does not excuse a crime. An old man is no less guilty because the years have passed.'

She saw that he was adamant and would not be moved from his purpose by any pleading on her part.

'Very well,' she said. 'If that is how you feel, so be it. I will say no more.'

He shot a keen glance at her, made suspicious perhaps by this sudden acquiescence. 'So you accept the situation as it is?'

'I accept that you must do whatever you feel you have to.'

'And you will not do anything foolish?'

'I? What can I do? It is for you to decide.'

'Yes,' he said. 'And I have decided.'

* * *

It was ten o'clock when she left the hotel. When she had told her father that she would be going out he had again looked at her with suspicion.

'Why do you have to do that?'

'Because I wish for a breath of fresh air. And also there are one or two things I wish to buy.'

'What things?'

'Toiletry. Nothing much. Have you any objection?'

She guessed that he was reluctant to let her go off on her own, knowing that she was not wholeheartedly with him in what he intended doing. It was obvious that he did not altogether trust her, and perhaps regretted that he had allowed her to see the pistols. Once those deadly weapons had been revealed it had no longer been possible to maintain with any degree of assurance that the meeting with Reedham was to be nothing but an exchange of talk. But he hesitated to put an outright ban on her outing; a ban which she might choose to ignore.

'I had rather you stayed here,' he said.

'Why? We do not leave until evening. I shall be back long before then.'

He might have protested that it was some time since he had enjoyed the company of his daughter and wished to make the most of it, but he did not. They would both have been aware of the insincerity of that argument, the relationship between them being as lacking in affection as it was.

'Well,' he said, 'don't be late. That is all.'

She assured him that she would not be, and went her way. She had racked her brains to think of a way out of her predicament, and one name had come up: Sam Grant. She would appeal to him. He would surely be able to advise her. And it would be a relief to share her problem with somebody else. She was surprised that she had not thought of this sooner; it was the obvious course of action. Immediately, even before speaking to him, the burden on her shoulders seemed lighter.

She could have telephoned from the hotel, but decided that it would be safer to use a public call-box. She found one some distance away and dialled the number which was entered in a notebook in her handbag. She heard the burr-burr of the ringing tone, and it seemed to go on for a long time. Oh please, she thought, let him be there, let him be there.

The burr-burr stopped; there was a click and then Sam Grant's voice: 'This is the Samuel Grant Inquiry Agency. Mr Grant is not available at present. If you would care to leave a recorded message please start speaking after the tone.'

She felt sick with disappointment. He was not there at the office. She had no idea where he might be, how long it would be before he returned. She rang off without leaving a message and left the call-box.

She killed time. She killed two hours before trying again. She listened to the burr-burr, praying: 'Please, Sam, be there now. Please! Please!'

'This is the Samuel Grant Inquiry Agency. Mr Grant is not available at present —'

'Oh God!'

*   *   *

They left the hotel at six o'clock. Neuberg rode in the front passenger seat as before, with Schroeder in the back. Gerda drove carefully through the London traffic, and it occurred to her that if she were to create an accident it might solve her problem. It would be easy enough; just a twist on the steering-wheel, a sudden pressure on the wrong pedal. But somehow she could not do it. An accident had to come without her contrivance; she had to rely on fate. And fate was not playing her game. They came out of London and on to the Hertfordshire road that would lead them to Maddenhall Superior and Marley Hall.

It was getting on for seven when they arrived at the gates. She stopped the car.

'This is it. Do you want me to drive up to the house?'

'No,' Neuberg said. 'You will wait here. Karl and I will walk the rest of the way.'

'How long will you be gone?'

'It should not take long to conclude our business.'

Once again his words had an ominous ring to them. It was all inevitable now; it was all going to happen and nothing could stop it. She wondered whether she would hear the shots from this distance. She had that feeling of nausea again. Even until this last moment she had still cherished a hope that some miracle might happen to avert the tragedy that was about to occur. But she knew now that there was to be no miracle. Even if it was not quite as it had been in the nightmare, it would be just as fatal. Reedham would be dead and she would have helped to kill him.

She sat in the car, and all around the darkness had closed in, sinister and foreboding. She crouched down on the seat, eyes shut, waiting for the sound of the shooting.

'Oh God! Oh dear God, help me!'

*　　*　　*

It was early evening when Grant and Cynara walked into the office in Shepherd's Bush. They had spent most of the day relaxing, the business being in the rather unprofitable state of lacking any clients currently on the books now that Gerda Hoffmann had settled her account and was no longer employing the agency. So they had paid a visit to the Tower of London, which, oddly enough, Cynara had never been to, and after a pleasant lunch in an Italian restaurant they had taken in a West End matinée and another meal to follow it.

It was Cynara who suggested that before going home they ought to look in at the office to find out whether there were any urgent messages from prospective clients that had been left in the answering machine.

'You never know. Something really big may have come up.'

'And pigs may fly.'

'Don't be so pessimistic,' she said. 'It's one of your worst failings. You should always look on the bright side.'

'When the sun's behind a cloud there isn't a bright side.'

He doubted whether what came out of the answering machine could have been described as bright either. It sounded distracted, as though the speaker was under a great deal of stress.

'Oh God, Sam! He's going to kill Reedham; I know it. I have to drive him out there this evening, and he's going to do it. He's got another man with him, and they've both got guns. Can you do something, Sam, please? Oh my God, I don't know when you'll be listening to this, and it may be too late. But please, Sam, please! I just don't know what to do. Please!'

She had not given her name, but of course there had been no need. There was only one person it could have been. They would have known even if they had not recognised the voice. She had sounded almost hysterical, and Grant had never known her to be like that; she had always seemed so cool and self-assured.

Cynara was looking deeply concerned. 'She's in trouble, Sam. She really is in trouble.'

'You don't need to tell me that. It's her father she's talking about, of course. He must have arrived in England and contacted her.'

'That's obvious. But do you think she can be mistaken? Do you think they really are going to kill Reedham?'

'Yes,' he said, 'I think she's dead right. It always did seem the most probable thing, even when she was bringing up all that stuff about Neuberg just wanting to confront him. Maybe she believed it herself then, but it was just not on the cards. This is a revenge thing.'

'So what are you going to do? This evening, she said. My God, it's evening already. They may be there right now.'

Grant did a quick think and came to a decision in ten seconds. 'I shall have to alert the Hertfordshire police.'

He had to get the number from Inquiries, and when he rang through a desk sergeant answered.

Grant spoke clearly and briefly. 'I have reason to believe a murder may be about to be committed at Marley Hall near a village named Maddenhall Superior. The victim's name is Clifford Reedham.'

'Just a minute,' the sergeant said. 'What is your name, sir?'

'Never mind my name. Send somebody out there at once. It's urgent. Even now it may be too late.'

He rang off.

'Will they do anything?' Cynara asked.

'God knows. They'll probably think it's a hoax. They get crackpots ringing up all the time. But they may be afraid to ignore it, because it might be genuine. Now I'd better be moving.'

'You're going out there?'

'You bet I'm going out there.'

'I'll come with you.'

'I thought you would,' he said.

* * *

Cragg went and opened the front door when the bell rang. A uniformed police constable in a peaked cap was standing in the porch. It was not the sort of person Cragg was ever happy to see, and he stared at the man with undisguised hostility.

'Yeah? What do you want?'

'I believe a Mr Reedham lives here.'

'So what if he does?'

'I'd like to have a word with him.'

'What about?'

'I'll tell him that when I see him. Is he in?'

Cragg thought of denying the fact, but then thought better of it. His instinct was always to lie to the police, but in this instance he came to the conclusion that it was hardly necessary. Neither he nor Reedham had committed any crime lately; not for years, in fact; so it was unlikely that either of them was about to be arrested. And he was curious to learn what this young fellow had to say.

'Well, yes, he is in. I'll go and tell him you're here.'

He lumbered away, and the police constable walked into the hall without further ado and was not far behind when Cragg opened the door of the drawing-room and said:

'There's a copper to see you.'

Reedham was sitting in one of his favourite places, an armchair by the fire, and he was visibly startled by this blunt announcement. He half rose from the chair before settling back again. The policeman came in, cap under arm. He looked boyish, possibly in his early twenties; fair-haired and snub-nosed.

'I won't keep you long, sir.'

He glanced at Cragg, waiting for him to leave. Cragg, correctly inferring that the officer would say nothing concerning the purpose of his visit while he was present, retired and closed the door.

'Won't you sit down, constable?' Reedham indicated a chair with a languid gesture.

'I'd rather stand,' the policeman said.

'As you wish. What is this all about?'

'Probably nothing at all, sir. Probably a hoax. But we have to follow these things up.'

'What things?'

'We had a telephone call at the station from a man who refused to give his name. The caller said that you were going to be murdered this evening.'

Reedham gave a start. 'Murdered! I?'

'That is what the man said. But like I told you, it was almost certainly a hoax. We do get these calls, Cranks, nutters. Do it for kicks, I suppose. But we have to take them seriously. You do understand, sir?'

Reedham had turned pale. The constable noticed it. It was as if he himself were really taking this thing seriously; as if he believed there was indeed a threat to his life.

'You don't know of anyone who would want to kill you, sir? I have to ask.'

Reedham shook his head. 'No. No one.' But of course he did. He knew very well. But that man was in Germany, not here. Or was he? What proof was there of that? He could be anywhere. And this person who had given the warning: who could he be? And how could he know so much?

'No old enemies?' the constable asked.

Reedham glanced at him sharply. What had put that thought into his head? Had it been intuition? Or did he know something? More than he was revealing, perhaps. Reedham was confused and frightened; really frightened.

'You say the man who made the call refused to give his name?'

'That's right. Rang off very quickly.'

'What did he sound like? Crazy?'

'I can't say, sir. I didn't take the call myself. You don't think he could have been genuine, do you, sir?'

'Oh, good lord, no.' Reedham tried to laugh but choked on the sound, as though he were being strangled. 'Who would want to kill me? I'm just a harmless old codger minding my own business and doing no harm to anyone. You said you often get hoaxers ringing up, didn't you?'

'Well, yes, occasionally.'

'And you can count on it this is another of them. Wasting your time, I'm afraid, officer.'

'It's something that goes with the job, sir.'

'I suppose so. Thank you all the same. I'm much obliged.'

FOURTEEN

Pay-Off

When the constable had driven away in his patrol car Cragg lost no time in coming to hear from Reedham's lips why the man had called. Reedham told him.

Cragg listened in silence until the story had been told; and then he said: 'You think Neuberg could be in this country and gunning for you?'

'What else am I to think, dammit?' Reedham's fear was making him testy. 'Who else would want to kill me?'

'Could be like the copper said. Just a hoax.'

'That would be a coincidence to beat the lot. Do you believe it was just that?'

Cragg shrugged. Reedham looked at his rugged face and could detect no sign of uneasiness there. Damn him! Why did he have to take it all so calmly? It was not as if he were not involved. He had been present on that fatal day in 1945. Neuberg had reason to hate him too, didn't he?

'He could be gunning for you too. You did some looting.'

'Sure I did. Who didn't in them days?' Cragg did a bit of scratching under his left arm, where he seemed to have an itch. 'What about this caller? Who do you think

179

it was? Always supposing it was on the level.'

Reedham had been thinking about that, and only one likely answer had come into his mind.

'The private eye.'

'You mean the guy what brought that there Miss Hoffmann to see you? Name of Grant, wasn't it?'

'Yes.'

'Why would he warn the coppers?'

'I don't know. But who else could it have been? Who else would have known anything about this business? I knew there was something wrong when they started asking about that damned picture, and when the girl wanted to know if I'd been in North Germany at the end of the War. The way I see it, she was doing some investigation for Neuberg and she'd got Grant to help her. I could see she didn't believe it when I told her I wasn't ever in that part of Germany. They didn't swallow my story about buying the picture in a junk shop either, if you ask me. And then I had to tell them I didn't report the theft to the police, and that was bound to look suspicious.'

'So now you think the girl has been in touch with Neuberg and put the finger on you, and he's over here and heading this way?'

'That's what it looks like.'

'I still don't see why Grant should alert the cops.'

'Maybe he got cold feet. Maybe he's only just found out what Neuberg is planning to do.'

'She wouldn't tell him that, would she?'

'How can we know what she'd do? It's all guesswork, isn't it? All just bloody guesswork. But there's one thing I'd bet on: that Neuberg is in England and coming here.'

'So what do you aim to do?'

Reedham started to get up from his chair. 'I've got to get away. Before it's too late.'

Cragg stepped towards him, put a hand on his shoulder and roughly pushed him back. 'That's no good. You start running and you're on the run for evermore.'

'But what else can I do?' Reedham's voice quavered.

'You can wait here and face the bastard. If you ask me, this talk of killing is all bullshit. He wants to take a look at you, sure. Maybe he'd like to put the fear of death into you. So he's done that already by the looks of things. Maybe he's even thinking of beating you up. But I'm here, ain't I? So it's not on.'

'Are you saying we should just wait for him?'

'You bet I am. If the man wants to cause trouble he'll get trouble; maybe more than he bargained for. We'll be ready for him. But running away. Oh no, that's not on.'

Reedham drew courage from Cragg's confidence. Perhaps he was right. Perhaps there really was nothing to fear.

'Maybe,' Cragg said, 'it was him what alerted the coppers. Just to scare the pants off you. Could be.'

* * *

Otto Neuberg and Karl Schroeder walked up the weedy drive towards Marley Hall side by side. There was a light in the porch, which guided them through the darkness, and they had no difficulty in finding the way. It was a dry night but overcast, and there was a slight breeze that made a faint soughing noise as it passed through the branches of the trees on either side. The only other sound was the crunching of their shoes on the gravel underfoot, for they were saying nothing.

They both knew what they had come to do, and there was no need for any last-minute discussion.

The front door was opened so promptly after Schroeder had rung the bell that it was almost as if the man who did so had been waiting in readiness for their arrival. It was Neuberg who spoke; Schroeder knew no English.

'We have come to see Mr Reedham.'

Cragg showed no surprise, though he had not been expecting two of them. It was a complication, but not too serious.

'Come in,' he said. 'Mr Reedham has been expecting you.'

It was Neuberg who had the surprise; this was something he had not foreseen. 'I think you are mistaken. Do you know who I am?'

Cragg gave a grin. 'Oh, yes. Mr Neuberg, ain't it?'

'Yes, but –'

'Well, don't just stand there. Come on in. I'll take you to him.'

Neuberg said something to Schroeder which Cragg could not understand, and both men stepped into the entrance hall. Cragg closed the door and led the way to the drawing-room where Reedham was waiting. He stood up when Cragg ushered the two visitors in. He also had been expecting only one man and was rather taken aback when he saw that there were two. It was all too apparent that he was nervous, but he was doing his best to appear at ease and play the welcoming host; though he did not offer to shake hands.

'Won't you sit down?' He indicated chairs well away from the one he had been sitting in, but facing it.

Neuberg sat down and Schroeder followed suit. Neuberg was trying to adjust to the situation, so different from what he had imagined it would be.

'You were expecting us?'

'I was expecting you,' Reedham said. 'You are Herr Neuberg?'

'Yes, I am Otto Neuberg.'

'And your companion?'

'Karl Schroeder. But how did you know I was coming?'

'Oh, let us not go into that.' Reedham had sat down again, while Cragg had closed the door and taken up a position behind him, standing. 'You don't mind if my man stays with us? He is, you might say, an interested party.'

Reedham was speaking smoothly, still nervous but gaining somewhat in confidence. He studied the two Germans, especially Neuberg. So this was what that boy had grown into. The face with the sabre scars touched no chord in his memory; he could see nothing of the boy in the grown man, fifty years on.

'How,' Neuberg asked, 'is he an interested party?'

'Oh, you don't know him? This is Arthur Cragg. Sergeant Cragg of the Wessex Rifles, as he was at the time.'

'Ah, the sergeant!'

Neuberg would not have recognised him. He would not have recognised Reedham either, and this disappointed him. He had come with the picture of that young officer in his mind, and here he was confronted by an old bald-headed man whom he did not know; a complete stranger. He felt as though he had been cheated. What satisfaction would there be in killing this dotard?

He said: 'I have been looking for you for half a century. You were a difficult man to find.'

'And in the end it was the painting that did it.

Bavarian Sunset. How odd. A little thing like that, taken on the spur of the moment. And you sent Miss Hoffmann to make inquiries. Why her?'

'It is Mrs Hoffmann, and she is my daughter. Who else should I have sent?'

'Ah, that explains it. And the reason why you wished to find me? What was that?'

'Do you need to ask?' Neuberg spoke with sudden anger. They had been sparring so far, but that was at an end. 'You cannot have forgotten what you did to my mother. Rape, assault, bestiality. Have you forgotten the state you left her in? Can't you imagine what effect that would have on a six-year-old boy?'

Reedham lost a little of his self-assurance. He had been lulled into a false sense of security during the initial exchanges, which had been without heat; just a sharing of information between two civilised persons. But suddenly the fire that had been smouldering beneath the surface had broken through into a blaze.

'I made a vow then,' Neuberg said. 'It was a vow to find and kill you, however long it might take. I have never renounced that vow.'

Some of the colour had receded from Reedham's cheeks. Fear was taking hold on him again; terror bubbling up inside. He made a move as if to get up from the chair, a wild idea in his mind of making a run for the door.

Neuberg spoke sharply: 'No!'

And now each of the visitors had a pistol in his hand. The weapons had come there as if by magic. It was obvious that they had been concealed under the jackets of the men; but now they were out in the open, black and steely and menacing.

Reedham subsided into the chair.

Cragg made a harsh inarticulate sound, started to move, saw the gun in Schroeder's hand pointing at him and stopped.

Neuberg said: 'That is better. As you see, we have come well prepared. Did you think we would be so foolish as to walk into this house unarmed?'

Reedham had not thought so. But while they had talked and neither of the visitors had made any aggressive move he had begun to believe that everything might be concluded peaceably; that Neuberg might just talk, perhaps accusingly, heaping abuse on him but nothing more. Now, however, he saw that this had been a vain expectation: Neuberg had come there for a purpose, and he had no intention of leaving without carrying it out. There was to be a killing, and he was the chosen victim. With the pistol pointing at him he began to plead for his life.

'No,' he said. 'You mustn't do it; you mustn't. It would be cold-blooded murder.'

'You may call it what you like. I prefer the word "execution". One long overdue.'

'And no trial? Is that fair? Is it right?'

'Was what you did fair or right? You speak of a trial. Well you have had it. In my mind. I have been witness for the prosecution and you have been judged guilty and sentenced to death. Have you any last words?'

Reedham began to babble. 'You cannot kill me. I beg you. I am an old man. I shall die soon anyway. What will you have gained? I beg you; I implore –'

Cragg glanced at him contemptuously. 'Don't grovel. Be a man. Don't bend your neck to a couple of bloody krauts.'

Neuberg lowered his pistol and looked at Cragg. 'So you would not do that? You are made of tougher material, eh?'

'You bet I am. I'm an old man too. I'm older than what he is. But I'd take you on any day, the two of us unarmed. Him as well.' He pointed at Schroeder. 'No quarter given and none asked.'

Neuberg's attention had been diverted from Reedham for the moment. It was a fatal mistake. Reedham was also armed; he had a snub-nosed revolver which had been in his possession many years, unlicensed and unused. After the departure of the policeman and his talk with Cragg he had dug it out, loaded it and put it in his pocket. While Neuberg had been covering him with the pistol he had been unable to pull it out; but now that Neuberg's gaze had wandered he saw his chance and seized it. His life was at stake and he did not hesitate: he drew the revolver and shot Neuberg in the chest, three times in quick succession.

Cragg, taking his cue from his employer, also moved into the attack. He had no gun but he had a long-bladed knife concealed on his person. He snatched it out now, and uttering a wild yell of defiance, made a rush at Schroeder. Schroeder shot him as he came, but the momentum of his rush carried Cragg forward in spite of the bullet in the chest. Schroeder was still seated in the chair and Cragg fell on him, thrusting the knife in one last effort into the German's throat.

* * *

Grant drove to Marley Hall at a speed which, after he had got himself free from the trammels of the London traffic, in places exceeded the legal limit. But there were no police cars around to pull him in, and he arrived at Marley Hall without mishap.

The first thing he saw was a white car parked by the entrance gate. Someone got out of it and ran towards his car as he came to a stop.

'It's Gerda,' Cynara said. 'The others must be at the hall.'

They had confirmation of this as soon as Gerda spoke. 'Oh, thank God you've come. I didn't know whether you'd get my message.' She sounded distracted. 'I've been nearly out of my mind. And even now it may be too late.'

'How long have they been gone?' Grant asked.

'Oh, quite some time. Well, it seems like it.'

'Jump in then. We'll drive up there.'

She got in and Grant drove through the gateway and on to the gravel.

'They're both armed, you know,' she said. 'Do you have a gun?'

'At the moment, no. We shall just have to try persuasion. The mere presence of others may have a calming effect. They'd hardly start shooting people in front of us.'

'I hope you're right,' she said. But she sounded none too convinced.

They came to the porch. Grant switched off the engine, and they were just getting out when they heard a sudden burst of firing coming from inside the house; four or five shots in rapid succession.

'Oh, my God!' Gerda cried. 'We're too late.'

She ran to the front door. It was not locked, and she pushed it open and went inside, Grant and Cynara close at her heels. As they entered the hall they heard a sound that was strangely blood-chilling: it was laughter; a kind of insane high-pitched giggle. It appeared to be coming from the room where they had had their interview with Reedham not so long ago.

'Come on,' Grant said. 'This way.'

He went to the door and opened it, and was shocked by what he saw in the room. There were two men slumped in armchairs looking horribly dead; one with a great patch of blood on his chest, the other with a long knife stuck in his neck and blood running down from the wound. A third man was lying on the floor and moaning. Grant recognised him as Arthur Cragg, and he appeared to be in a bad way. He was also bleeding from the chest and more blood was trickling from his mouth. The other two men were strangers to Grant, but he guessed that one was Otto Neuberg and the other had to be the companion he had brought with him.

Gerda and Cynara had also come into the room and were gazing in horror at this scene of carnage.

It was Reedham, of course, who had been doing the laughing; but he had stopped when Grant and the others had entered the room. He alone appeared to be uninjured; there was a revolver in his hand and he was waving it about in what seemed to Grant to be a highly dangerous manner.

'Come in,' he shouted. 'Come in, all of you. Everybody welcome. Come and take a look.'

'Don't you think you'd better put that gun down?' Grant said. 'You could do some more damage, and it seems to me there's been enough done already.'

'What?' Reedham said. He glanced at the revolver, as if only then realising that it was still in his hand. 'Oh yes, of course. No need for it any more.' He laid it on the mantelpiece. 'It's done its job. Look at him.' He pointed at Neuberg's dead body. 'He came to kill me, but I killed him instead. Isn't that a joke, eh?' He went off into another fit of the giggling laughter. 'Came to take his revenge, and what did he get? A bullet in the heart.

Now it's all over; I don't have to worry about him any more. I'm free, free.'

He noticed Gerda standing there, glancing from him to her dead father and back again.

'Why, if it isn't Miss Hoffmann. Or should I say Mrs Hoffmann? Yes, he told me. Your father. You've been bereaved, my dear. Too bad. You shouldn't have got involved. It was your own fault and you've only yourself to blame. Well, he's not much bloody loss, if you ask me.'

Her self-control gave way at this; it was the goading that did it. She might not have had any deep affection for her father, but this was too much. This was the man who had raped and half-killed her grandmother; this was the monster who had escaped retribution for fifty years and now was gloating because he had killed the one person who would have put the record straight. Once again he had got away with it.

He seemed to catch the expression in her eyes, and even in his near-hysterical state it disconcerted him. He began to excuse himself.

'You don't have to look at me like that. I only did what I had to do. He had a gun. He was going to shoot me. He said so. A man's entitled to kill in self-defence; that's the law.'

Yes, she thought; it was the law, and that was how he would plead. And they would let him off, let him go free. He was never going to be made to pay, never.

'No,' she murmured, 'no, no, no!'

Neuberg's pistol was lying on the carpet where it had fallen from his hand. She needed to take only two steps to reach it. She snatched it up and pointed it at Reedham.

His eyes widened. 'No!'

'Yes!' she said. 'Yes!'

She pressed the trigger and shot him between the eyes.

FIFTEEN

A Kind of Revenge

It was months since it had all happened, and they were in the Peak District. It had been Cynara's suggestion.

'You need a holiday, Sam.'

He was not so sure about that. He had not really been overworked lately; there had not been enough clients for that. But maybe a holiday would not be such a bad idea. And maybe they could afford it. Just.

And then she had come up with this idea of the Peaks. Which was maybe all very fine for her, because she was young and vigorous and would probably take all that climbing in her stride. He was not so young and maybe not quite so vigorous. His idea of a holiday was more the lying round in the sun variety; but if she wanted the Peaks, okay she had better have them. And he had to admit that the views were magnificent, and probably worth all the toil of getting to them.

They were trying to forget what had happened at Marley Hall. But of course it was impossible completely to forget something like that: the blood and the carnage. It remained printed indelibly on the memory.

Cragg had survived, though it had been touch and go with him for a time. Moreover, it was probable that no charges would be brought against him, for he had surely acted in self-defence; the bullet in his chest was evidence of that. There were rumours too that his story of events, right from that initial incident in Germany, which was to have such fatal consequences, was being ghost-written for a popular newspaper, and that he would receive a whacking great fee. Which was all very nice for him, and probably a lot more than he deserved.

Gerda's trial had not yet come up. Grant hoped that the courts would treat her leniently, bearing in mind the extreme provocation and the fact that her crime had not been premeditated.

It was Cynara's opinion that she ought to be let off altogether. 'That swine, Reedham, deserved shooting. He was a thoroughly bad lot from start to finish.'

'No doubt he was. But you can't just go round shooting people simply because they're bad lots.'

'More's the pity,' Cynara said.

* * *

On one of the wet days they took shelter in a stately home that was open to the public. It belonged to a nobleman who had to make a bit of money in this way to help pay for the upkeep of the building.

They were in the long gallery looking at the pictures when Cynara gave a sudden cry of amazement.

'Oh, my God! Look at that!'

She was pointing and Grant looked at the object indicated. He went nearer and looked more closely. There was a brass plate below the picture and on it he read: 'Bavarian Sunset by Arnold Sempler 1905-42'.

'Well, well, well!' he said. 'So this is where it went to.'

It was a pleasant enough painting, but not, he would

have thought, in any way remarkable. Nor did it look at all decadent; so it must have been his Jewishness rather than his art that had sent Arnold Sempler to his death in the concentration camp.

But the picture had been responsible for other deaths since then, and two of the victims had been neo-Nazis. So maybe you could say that Sempler had had a kind of revenge in the end. And perhaps he was laughing now. Wherever he was.